TRUE SON

SON

Lana Krumwiede

CANDLEWICK PRESS

Copyright © 2015 by Lana Krumwiede

First edition 2015

Library of Congress Catalog Card Number 2014945451
ISBN 978-0-7636-7262-1

15 16 17 18 19 20 BVG 10 9 8 7 6 5 4 3 2 1

Printed in Berryville, VA, U.S.A.

This book was typeset in Berkeley Oldstyle Medium.

Candlewick Press
99 Dover Street
Somerville, Massachusetts 02144

visit us at www.candlewick.com

For all the readers who asked
what happened next

• • •

NAU MILITARY INTEL ADMIN LOGBOOK 9.14.256

> Communication 5489v210/487 confirms the existence of
certain Class J Abnormalities [*Handbook of Operations,*
Appendium 4, p. 1391] observed in Foreign Sector #187. <

> Local Combat Overseer Harbock W. Rezzine IX [ID#
70-3692-261] filed Action Request Form recommending
Aggression Procedure 23, Category V. <

> Approval pending. <

I GEVRI

At the Ohandai defense facility near the northern bor-
der of the Republik, Gevri had risen earlier than anyone
else in his unit—all but Jix, that is. The jaguar padded
silently at his side as they climbed the spiral steps to
the top of the north watchtower. Last winter, Gevri had
almost lost her when he had tried to escape to the city
of Deliverance. Gevri shuddered. Thank gods he was over
his idiotic obsession with Nathan's City. What a disaster
that had been!

"We got through it—that's what counts." Gevri reached down to stroke Jix's ear, and the big cat responded with a soft chuffing noise. Life was infinitely better now that Gevri had embraced his role as an archon, a soldier of the Republikite army trained in the use of dominion—or psi, as it was called in Nathan's City. He was ashamed to think of how he had once fought against his destiny, how he had turned his back on his own father, believing that dominion shouldn't be used as a weapon. But that was before Gevri had realized how untrustworthy the people of Nathan's City were. For the first time, Gevri understood why his father, General Sarin, had pushed him as hard as he had. The general had wanted to prepare his son for the real world—a world in which every person looked out for himself, whether Republikite, Nathanite, or Nau.

Now that Gevri had changed his ways, his father treated him with a new level of respect, even giving him command of a special archon strike force that was the talk of the entire military. They'd been sent to Ohandai on a critical mission, and his father had made it clear that the stakes had never been higher. For decades, the Republik had been at war with the neighboring Nau, who kept using advanced technology to defeat the Republikite army at nearly every turn, advancing farther and farther into Repulikite territory. Now, however, the Republik was preparing to counter the assault with a force unlike any the Nau had ever seen: an elite force of archons trained in the use of telekinetic warfare.

Stepping onto the top of the watchtower that overlooked the Ohandai foothills, Gevri squinted in the light of daybreak. The sentry stationed at the watchtower turned to him with an outward palm, the proper salute for a ranking officer.

Gevri returned the salute with a downward palm. "Anything unusual?"

"No, sir," the soldier replied. "A quiet night, sir." He turned away from Gevri as quickly as etiquette allowed, clenching his jaw and tightening his grip on the rifle. Gevri turned to look at the other soldiers posted at the watchtower and sensed the same nervous tension. Some of it must be due to Jix. Even though she was perfectly behaved, people just weren't used to being this close to a cat who could crush a man's skull in a heartbeat. But Gevri could guess what was really troubling the soldiers: being this close to an archon.

The archons were the only soldiers who had the

psychic abilities known as dominion. After being kept secret for years, the archon units had been introduced to the regular troops a few months ago. Though the regular soldiers were under orders to accept the archons, most were uncomfortable being around people with dominion. Telekinesis—the ability to move and manipulate objects with the mind—didn't sit well with them. They were even less comfortable around Gevri's unit, whose archons were the only ones who had other, rarer forms of dominion such as telepathy (the ability to read minds) and remote viewing (the ability to see things many miles from where you stood). While Gevri understood the soldiers' discomfort, he knew that once they saw how helpful dominion was in battle, they would embrace the archons.

Gevri walked along the wall of the watchtower. He'd never been this far west and north before; the climate was much drier than his hometown of Kanjai. It had been dark when his transport had arrived last night, and this morning he was eager to get a sense of the land.

Sweeping his gaze over the horizon, he saw very few trees. The hills were covered with wild grasses and shrubs. The late summer had turned the rolling hills a golden color that made him think of sand dunes. His military training took over as he surveyed the ripples and folds of the land. If a small group of soldiers wanted to hide from the sentries, they would have plenty of places to choose from. "That's why we're here," Gevri whispered to Jix.

The jaguar stretched her legs out and lowered her head. It was her way of saying she was eager for action, ready for anything.

Ten days earlier, the Nau army had launched a full-blown attack on the Ohandai defense facility. Gevri and his strike force had been far away, assisting in the skirmishes in the northern lake region, but he'd heard about the surprise attack and the heavy losses. The Republikites managed to repel the Nau and hold the facility, but Ohandai wasn't out of danger yet. The facility was in desperate need of supplies and reinforcements, which would take at least another week to arrive. In the meantime, Ohandai was vulnerable. The Nau could very well send in a small strike force of its own and breach the gates of the weakened facility. It was Gevri's job to make sure that didn't happen.

A wave of confidence swelled inside him. His unit was perfectly suited for this mission. Though they were all young—just kids, really—they had been chosen because of their rare powers: clairvoyance, remote viewing, psychometry, telepathy, and retrocognition. It was funny to think that it had taken an infidel from Nathan's City to bring these archons' talents to light; before the arrival of the Nathanite Taemon, these young archons had been thought powerless because they didn't exhibit the usual form of dominion, telekinesis. But thanks to Taemon, everyone knew of their rare and extraordinary gifts—and General Sarin knew just what to do with them.

The general had begun developing dominion in young soldiers when Gevri was born. At seventeen, Gevri was the oldest archon by a good five years, the first one the general had trained. In addition to telekinesis, Gevri had telepathy. As far as anyone knew, he was the only archon with *two* forms of dominion—a fact of which his father was especially proud.

Gevri's team might be young, but the special archon strike force was skilled. They were trained. And they would not fail.

Six days later, Gevri and his team knew the layout of the Ohandai facility from stem to stern. They had repelled several attacks already, and it was obvious what the enemy was targeting: the transmissions room, the power generator, and the watchtowers. He'd split the archons into groups of two and three to make sure all three targets were defended. The strategy had succeeded so far, but Gevri knew enough to guard himself from over-confidence. One mistake could mean losing the entire facility to the Nau.

The Nau. Two hundred years ago, nine of the most powerful nations of the world had united into one super-nation and divided the world into nine regions, each overseen by one of the nine powers. One by one, nations had capitulated to the Nau. Two centuries later, only a few places still stubbornly clung to their independence, and the Republik was one of them. Sometimes it seemed like the Nau had endless resources, but their weakness was in their size. They had endless regulations and pro-cedures to maintain, which meant they weren't exactly nimble. They took a long time to decide where to attack, but once they attacked, they could be deadly. So far, the Republik had managed to remain independent despite Nau persuasions. But in the past decade, the Nau had gradually stepped up their aggression, and the Republik was on the verge of defeat. Losing the Ohandai facility could be the last straw for the resistance to which Gevri's family had devoted many lifetimes.

Reinforcements from the Republikite army were due to arrive at Ohandai tonight. If Gevri's team could keep the facility safe for a few more hours, the mission would be a success. But surely the Nau knew that as well. They would mount another attack today; Gevri was certain of it.

Today, Gevri's position was on the north watchtower. With him were two other archons, Pik and Mirtala, along with half a dozen regular soldiers on sentry rotation. The sentries kept their distance from the archons, which was fine with Gevri. His unit operated independently.

Pik, who had been using his remote viewing to locate the enemy, took off his glasses to wipe the dust from them.

"I think it's funny that a remote viewer needs glasses," Mirtala said.

"Remote viewing has nothing to do with eyesight."

"I know," she said. "But it's still funny."

Gevri changed the subject. "Any luck?" he asked Pik.

"No, sir," Pik replied.

Mirtala screwed up her face in disgust. "You've been up here four hours. Seems like you could've found them by now."

A few months ago, Pik would have been insulted by Mirtala's backtrash. But now, the team had gelled and everyone knew this was Mirtala's way of motivating her teammates.

"Have you ever tried to look *everywhere*?" Pik said. "It takes a long time. It would help if I knew what direction to look in or at what distance—some way to focus my dominion."

Mirtala grunted and folded her arms.

"Keep trying," Gevri said, and made a mental note to give Pik a break soon. Four hours was pushing the fatigue point for remote viewing. He directed his next order to the jaguar. "Go down there and scout around for us, Jix. See if you can pick up on their scent, or anything that might give us a clue where they are."

Jix turned and disappeared down the stairwell. She understood Gevri's commands through her own animal version of dominion. In fact, Gevri didn't need spoken words to communicate with Jix; they'd developed a telepathic link some time ago. But using words helped Gevri form his ideas more clearly—and it put others at ease—so he used them when he could.

It was time to check in with Saunch, who was guarding

the transmissions station with Berliott, another remote viewer. Gevri pictured Saunch in his mind, formed the telepathic link, and sent his thoughts: *Has Berliott found anything yet?*

Nothing. Gevri heard Saunch's voice clearly in his mind. *Maybe they've given up?*

I doubt it, Gevri replied. *I have a feeling they'll try one last time before the reinforcements get here.*

I would if I were them, Saunch answered.

Exactly. Stay sharp. Tell Berliott that Jix is out scouting. Hopefully we'll have something to report soon.

Yes, sir.

A few minutes later, another message came to Gevri's mind, but it wasn't from Saunch. This message came as an image rather than as words. He'd tried to teach the other telepaths how to communicate with images, and they could do it, but words still came more easily to them. Beyond that, this message had an entirely different flavor, which was the best way Gevri could describe it. The image that came to him was lush and wild and raw, and it could only be from Jix. She'd found something.

Jix was showing Gevri a cluster of discarded equipment:

a helmet. An equipment bag. A mess kit. It looked like someone had left in a hurry and forgotten a few things.

Now Jix was sending him scents: tobakk, the kind the Nau soldiers all smoked. And now urine. *Gods, Jix! Enough smells!* Gevri couldn't help covering his nose, even though he knew the scents were only in his brain.

The next images were landmarks, which helped Gevri figure out where Jix had found these things. *Good work.*

Gevri turned to Pik, who was still trying to locate the enemy with his remote viewing, and pointed in the direction of Jix's discovery. "Check over there Jix found something."

"Yes, sir."

If he could recover the items Jix had found, Mirtala might be able to glean more information from them. She was the only archon whose dominion manifested as psychometric ability, which allowed her to touch an object and know who had used it, how they had used it, and what they had been feeling at the time.

If Gevri had been able to see the items with his own eyes, he'd be able to use telekinesis to transport them. But the image Jix had sent him was not strong enough

to create the psychic connection required for telekinesis. He'd need to send someone out to retrieve the items.

Gevri created a telepathic connection with Neeza, who was stationed at the power generator. *Neeza?*

Sir? came Neeza's tiny voice. Her telepathic messages mirrored her speaking voice, which was quiet and shy.

Jix found some equipment left behind by the enemy. I need you and Wendomer to go find it and bring it to the watchtower so Mirtala can do a reading. But don't touch anything. Have Wendomer check it out with clairvoyance. It could be rigged.

Rigged? Neeza asked. *You mean like booby-trapped?*

It could be. If Gevri had learned anything from his trip to Deliverance, it was this: count on your enemy to lie and trick you at every turn. Taemon and all the people of Nathan's City had taken deception to despicable lengths. Someday Gevri would return to Deliverance and settle that score, but for now, he had to stay focused on this mission.

Just be careful, he told Neeza. *Check back with me after Wendomer has a good look.* Gevri sent Neeza the same images of the landmarks that Jix had sent him.

We'll find it, sir. We're leaving right now.

Be quick, Gevri added. Sending Neeza and Wendomer to collect the equipment meant Cindahad would be the lone archon at the power generator, which was a risk. But it wouldn't take long to collect the items, and Mirtala might be able to extract valuable information from them. He couldn't pass up this opportunity to learn what the Nau were up to. Besides, it wasn't as if Cindahad would be *completely* alone. There were a few regular soldiers stationed at the power generator.

The next few minutes seemed to drag on forever, and Gevri was feeling more uncomfortable with each one. Pik still couldn't locate the Nau soldiers, but Gevri was certain they were out there. Mirtala was restless. Neeza hadn't checked in yet. Jix had been silent since finding the supplies. Gevri felt reluctant to send any telepathic messages, since an ill-timed message could be startling at a moment when concentration is needed.

Finally Neeza's voice came to his mind. *Lieutenant Gevri, sir?*

Yes. Your report, Neeza?

We found the items, sir. We haven't touched them, but Wendomer senses nothing out of the ordinary. Permission to transport the items to your location, sir?

Gevri hesitated. Why were those things left out there? Such an amateur mistake seemed very unlike the Nau. And yet even professionals made mistakes. Gevri's job was to make use of them. *Have Wendomer check one more time. Report back.*

Yes, sir.

Gevri could picture Wendomer staring at the helmet, the equipment bag, and the mess kit, but it was just his imagination. If he had clairvoyance, like Wendomer — and the Nathanite Taemon — he would have been able to sense things about objects that were not visible or knowable by any of the five standard senses. He wouldn't have to send his soldiers out to find things for him. It wasn't from lack of trying that Gevri didn't have clairvoyance, though. Once the general discovered these rare forms of dominion and realized that Gevri already possessed telepathy, Gevri had been subjected to every kind of —

Wendomer says they're clean, sir. Permission to transport the items?

Bring them in, Gevri told her.

Gevri glanced at his watch. Pik had been exercising dominion past his optimum duration. "As soon as we get those two back inside the compound, you can take a break," he said. "But right now, I'd feel a lot better if you could tell me where those enemy soldiers are."

Pik nodded. "I'll find them, sir."

"Sometime this decade would be nice," Mirtala added.

Jix. Gevri reached out to the jaguar. *Got anything else for me?*

A vague feeling came back from Jix, which Gevri took to mean "Not really."

"So that's where you are," Pik murmured. "Closer than I thought."

The dreamy tone of Pik's voice triggered a sinking feeling in Gevri. "Where? Where are they, Pik?"

When the boy didn't respond, Gevri shook him by the shoulder. "Pik! You're overextending. Break the connection. That's an order. Break the connection!"

"Clever little demons, all of you. Watch out, Neeza!" Pik's unfocused stare and wide pupils told Gevri everything. Pik had allowed too much of his awareness to drift far outside of himself. He had lost the connection with his immediate physical surroundings. It was a dangerously vulnerable position for a remote viewer: Pik couldn't hear, see, or feel anything near him. In a few minutes, physical fatigue would set in and Pik would fall into a deep sleep. It was the body's natural defensive reaction.

I pushed him past his limits, Gevri thought as Neeza and Wendomer came into sight, carrying the supplies. *Now I've lost my remote viewer.* He should have rotated his team earlier, but there was no time for crying over a tipped bucket. He had to keep it together. He had to get Neeza and Wendomer back into the compound before the Nau got to them.

Neeza! Wendomer! Drop the items right now and run!

Yes, sir.

Without another word, the two young archons did as they were told. The helmet, the mess kit, and the bag were left behind as they sprinted toward the gate that led to the watchtower.

Gevri took a deep breath and glanced at the other soldiers stationed as sentries on the watchtower. What he was about to do would baff them out, but they were going to have to live with it.

Focusing his gaze on the three items, Gevri tapped into his telekinetic powers and ordered each of the objects to relocate. In a matter of seconds, the helmet, mess kit, and bag lifted from the ground, floated through the air, and came to rest at his feet.

"Time to do your thing, Mirtala," Gevri said, ignoring the gasps and murmurs of the nearby soldiers. He turned to check on Pik, and sure enough, the boy was snoring like a lumbersaw. If he'd been out in the field, it could have been a problem to be so defenseless. But here, inside the compound and surrounded by his team, Pik would be fine until he woke up in an hour or two. Gevri eased the boy's glasses off his nose and slipped them into his shirt pocket.

Mirtala crouched over the helmet. She hung her head and closed her eyes, moving her hand gracefully across its surface. "Hostility. Anger. Resentment. The man who wore this was a talented artist. Then he was forced to become a soldier. He blamed it all on the Republik."

"Tell me where he is right now," Gevri said, trying to control the urgency in his voice.

When Mirtala lifted her head, tears welled in her eyes. "He's dead," she said. "And his paintings were beautiful."

"I'm sorry." And he *was* sorry. Sorry that an artist was dead. Sorry that Mirtala had to feel that. Sorry about all that muck, but the Ohandai could still fall if his team failed. He took the helmet from Mirtala and handed her the bag. "Try this."

Watching Mirtala's face, he saw her features relax and sensed that she had forced the grief into a place where it would have to be dealt with later. Gevri tried to remember how old Mirtala was. Eleven? Ten, maybe? A strange combination of sadness and pride washed over him.

"Oh. This could be helpful," Mirtala said. "It's a communication device. They transmitted orders with this thing."

"What were the orders?" Gevri asked.

Head tilted sideways, Mirtala concentrated. "Just a minute . . ."

Neeza and Wendomer came to the top of the stairway, panting and looking worried.

"Are they out there?" Wendomer said. "Did you see them?"

"I can't see them, but I know they're out there somewhere. Pik saw them. Mirtala is about to —"

"Gods' aid," Mirtala said, her voice strained with fear. "These things were planted as a distraction to draw us away. The plan is to attack the power generator!"

A sick feeling shuddered down Gevri's spine. It was just as he'd feared.

NAU MILITARY INTEL ADMIN LOGBOOK 9.27.256

> Investigation Order 369/34 issued by Regional
Combat Overseer Gildress P. Coppen Jr. [TD# 201-5790-
628] concerning Class J Abnormalities [*Handbook of
Operations*, Appendium 4, p. 1391] observed in Foreign
Sector #187. <

> Military Investigator U. Felmark Puster [ID# 229-
8831-305] assigned as Lead Field Researcher. <

2 TAEMON

Summer was in its glory on Mount Deliverance. The sun warmed Taemon's shoulders through the rough cotton fabric of his shirt. Insect sounds thrummed in the trees. Taemon walked through the dry grass that came up to his knees. He could have walked on the path, but then he would've missed the way the grass whispered to him as he parted it with long strides.

He was alone with his mountain in the summer. All was right.

Amma had wanted to come with him, but he needed this solitude. She had offered to wait for him at the bottom of the trail, but he'd begged her not to. Even the thought of someone waiting for him would interrupt the freedom he needed right now. The freedom to open his mind to the Heart of the Earth. The freedom to set all other cares aside and commune with the world he belonged to.

He emptied his mind and focused on the feel of the grass against his legs. The give of the soil beneath each footstep. The call and answer of birdsong.

Taemon had lost track of how far he'd walked, but when he came to a huge ruddybark tree—the trunk was wider than a quadrider—he stopped.

He settled himself in the mossy ground next to the enormous tree, stretching out on his back and gazing into the leafy abyss above him. How old was this tree? Had it been here when the prophet Nathan had pulled the mountain out of the earth to separate Deliverance from the rest of the world?

Taemon had often thought about his ancestor Nathan, the first one to be given psi by the Heart of the Earth. How much power did it take to create a mountain? Nathan would have had to envision every surface, every crevice, every streambed, every valley and ridge, then have held that vision in his head as he sent an unfathomable amount of psionic power into the earth's surface. And what about the plant life? Had Nathan envisioned each tree and flower and meadow as well? Or had that come later? Maybe this very tree had been envisioned and created by Nathan himself.

I am the creator of trees and meadows, a voice said in Taemon's mind. **By my consent, others are allowed to take part in creation.**

It used to bother him, hearing her voice like that, but now the familiarity of it was a comfort. This is why he had come, to speak to the Heart of the Earth.

I've done my best, Taemon replied. *I've tried very hard. But I've made a mess of things.* While Taemon had managed to scare off an initial attack by the Republikite army through tricks and a surprising display of psi, he had no doubt that the army would attempt a second attack at some point. Perhaps they'd even realize that the people of Deliverance were powerless and that Taemon's show had been just that—a show. *I didn't anticipate any of that when I took psi away from Deliverance.*

One cannot possibly anticipate all outcomes, the

Heart of the Earth replied. **You chose what was needed at the time.**

Taemon closed his eyes and let his awareness sink into the earth below him, the tree next to him, the birds above him, the air that surrounded him. He was a part of this earth. He'd been given the gift of power and authority over it. He'd made one decision; now he would make another.

He began gathering psi, felt it swell and multiply within him. He was no longer bound by the limitations of his body. He was as large as a mountain, as deep as the sea, as vast as the sky. It pulsed and rippled and crashed through him. It was time. Time to form the words.

Let all psi be done away with. Not only in Deliverance, but in all countries, lands, and peoples of this earth. Let all power to direct creation be returned to the Heart of the Earth. Let every man, woman, and child learn to trust the earth and live by her grace and goodness. Be it so!

The swell of psi left him, and yet he was not at peace. Something was not right. He felt an emptiness, a great void. The Heart of the Earth had not granted his request.

The emptiness that filled him prevented any anguish or tears over this failure.

Am I not the True Son? Taemon asked. *Is that over, and am I just me again?* Part of him hoped that was true.

You are the True Son for the People of Deliverance, said the Heart of the Earth. You were chosen to act on their behalf. Your authority does not include the right to dictate the fate of those outside of Deliverance.

In that case, Deliverance is doomed, Taemon thought.

Your work is not finished. You will yet act on behalf of the people of Deliverance.

Taemon wanted to groan. How was he supposed to save his people when he was the only one with psi? His life had become a never-ending series of impossible tasks.

More is possible than you know, were the Heart of the Earth's parting words.

That much was true. Two years ago, would Taemon ever have imagined he could turn Deliverance into a powerless city? Or travel to the Republik? Or turn back an army of archons? None of those things had seemed possible, either.

But still, save the people of Deliverance? It was too much to ask. After all that had happened, it was too much. He lay still for a while longer, lingering under the protection of the ancient tree, staring into the green canopy and thinking about anything other than his latest impossible duty.

Gevri's face came to his mind again. He'd first met Gevri on the Republik side of this very mountain. Taemon and Amma had crossed through the mountain to rescue Taemon's da, and Gevri had been running away from his own father, General Sarin. He and Gevri had started off as friends. Well, maybe not friends, exactly, but allies. Now they were enemies, at least in Gevri's mind.

Taemon thought about all the choices, large and small, he'd made on that journey. What should he have done differently? Should he have trusted Gevri from the start, confided in him about Deliverance's powerlessness? Amma had urged him to be open with Gevri, but Taemon had insisted that they keep the truth from him. It was too big a secret to entrust to a stranger—especially one from the Republik. But if Taemon had leveled with Gevri, they might have avoided the huge blowup when Gevri finally learned that Taemon had lied. And Gevri might still be their ally—rather than a leader in the enemy army.

And then there were the archons he'd met and trained in the Republik: Saunch, Pik, Berliott, Wendomer, Cindahad, Mirtala, and Neeza. They had been a group of castoffs when he'd met them. The archon army had all but given up on them. Taemon had showed them the value of their unusual powers, and they had helped him escape. They had begged to come with him, but Taemon had refused. The trip had been too dangerous even for children with their skills—and he couldn't guarantee a welcome reception by the people of Deliverance, who would likely feel threatened by a group of Republikite children with dominion. But what had happened to these young archons? Had Gevri and General Sarin punished them for the roles they played in his escape?

Perhaps Taemon should never have gone to the Republik in the first place. Skies, enough people had tried to talk him out of it before he left. But someone had to rescue Da (or, as it turned out, Uncle Fierre). Taemon was certain that his uncle would be dead by now if not for Taemon and Amma's trip across the mountain. In spite of its consequences, he refused to think of the journey as a mistake.

When the dappled sunlight began to dim, Taemon knew he had to go. Lying here any longer would solve nothing. It was time to go back to Deliverance and figure out how to save his people—again.

By the time he reached the west gate that led to the city, the sun had nearly set. The guards knew him by now and let him through without a fuss.

Only a few steps past the gate, Amma rushed toward him and grabbed his arm. "Thank the Skies you're back," she said. "Hurry! There's something you have to see."

> Documentation Update filed by Local Combat Overseer
Harbock W. Rezzine IX [ID# 70-3692-261] recommending
changes in classification of Class J Abnormalities
[Handbook of Operations, Appendium 4, pp. 1387-1465].
Approval pending. <

> Request for Clarification filed by Military
Investigator U. Felmark Puster [ID# 229-8831-305]. <

3 GEVRI

Gevri fumbled with the communications device. He had to press it three times before he hit the right knob. Telepathy was so much quicker, but two-way communication only worked with other telepaths.

"Lieutenant Sarin to Commander Vichan. Send reinforcements to the generator immediately! Imminent attack!"

The handheld device crackled with static before the response came. "Commander Vichan to Lieutenant Sarin. Acknowledged."

Gevri was not about to count on the commander's forces to protect Cindahad. They were stretched thin as it was, with a slim chance of getting additional soldiers to the generator in time to defend it. Could the few soldiers already at the generator handle a Nau attack? As powerful as Cindahad's remote viewing was, it was not a useful skill in close combat. That, and she was only nine years old.

Cindahad was in trouble, and Gevri wasn't going to let her down.

"Wendomer, you're coming with me. Neeza, you stay here with Mirtala. Keep your mind open for my messages." Gevri turned and bolted for the stairway, catching Neeza's "Yes, sir" over his shoulder. Wendomer was right behind him.

On the way down the stairs, Gevri sent a message to Saunch. *The Nau are going to attack the generator. Cindahad is there, but Wendomer and I are on the way. I need Berliott to locate the Nau. Then you relay that information to me.*

Yes, sir.

Gevri burst out of the door at the bottom of the tower and pulled up short. Wendomer rammed into him from behind, shoving Gevri within three inches of colliding with a Nau probot. About the size of a barstool, these little nasties were sent in to collect images of enemy territory. They could defend themselves, too, but they were only accurate within a short range. And three inches definitely qualified as short range.

Gevri reacted quickly by using dominion to slice the probot in two. Then, when the transmission light on the top half of the probot continued to glow, he brought a handy rain barrel down to smash it. Twice.

"It's destroyed, sir," Wendomer said. "Thoroughly."

Gevri nodded. Where were the soldiers stationed at this door? No time to look for them. He ran on.

He pulled up short again when he came to a blind corner and stretched an arm behind him to stop Wendomer. Side by side, they pressed against the cold concrete wall. He could hear gunfire ahead. Gunfire and grinding engine sounds.

"Sounds like a fat pig," he whispered to Wendomer. The small, agile fighting vehicles had earned the name fat pigs from their front gun barrel, which resembled a pig's snout.

"Confirmed," whispered Wendomer. "One fat pig, two soldiers inside."

How had the Nau managed to get a fat pig inside the compound? Gods, this was bad.

Sir, Berliott's found them. It was Saunch. And not a nick too soon.

Where? Gevri asked.

There are fourteen Nau soldiers in the compound. Seven of them are in the anteroom to the generator, preparing explosives. Three are trying to break into the armory. Two are in the warehouse. And two are inside a fat pig just outside the generator building. He could feel the anxiety in Saunch's message.

Gevri radioed the commander and relayed the locations.

"Lieutenant Sarin," the commander responded, "twelve soldiers are on their way to the generator. They are not equipped, I repeat, *not equipped,* to go up against a fat pig."

"My team'll take care of the pig," Gevri said. "You send those soldiers to the armory and the warehouse."

"What about the seven inside the generator room? And the explosives?"

"We've got those, too," Gevri said. *I hope.*

Jix, where are you?

No response came, but Jix played by her own rules sometimes. Gevri couldn't afford to wait. He whispered the plan to Wendomer. "I'll take out the fat pig, then you and I have to take back the generator building. Where's Cindahad? Can you sense her?"

Wendomer nodded. "She's hiding in the generator room, sir. The seven are still working on the explosives in the anteroom."

"First things first," Gevri said. "We've got a pig to roast." Leaning around the corner just far enough to spot the fat pig, he stared at the fighting vehicle. It pivoted in front of the generator entrance, its tracks grinding on the concrete and its snout spitting bullets at anything that moved. Gevri focused on the bottom of the fighting vehicle, the floor of the compartment where the two soldiers sat. He began heating the metal, pouring more and more dominion into it until he heard a shrill, metallic *skreeeek*.

Wendomer chuckled. "The fat pig is squealing."

"Those Nau soldiers can't last much longer," Gevri said.

Sure enough, the hatch on top of the pig flew open and the two soldiers jumped out, running for cover. They didn't get far; Gevri used dominion to yank their boots and send the soldiers sprawling. Once on the ground, he restricted their air flow until they passed out, then used their own bootlaces to truss their hands and feet.

"Let's move," Gevri said. He and Wendomer ran past the fat pig, now idle, and stopped beside the door of the generator building. He pressed himself as flat as possible against the front wall, staying a few feet away from the door, and motioned for Wendomer to do the same.

As soon as Gevri opened the door with dominion, bullets exploded out of the doorway. As expected, someone was covering the door. He signaled Wendomer to scoot away from the door, and they shuffled around the corner until they were against the side wall.

"Ready?" Gevri whispered.

Wendomer replied with a solemn nod.

Gevri blasted dominion into the concrete wall, creating a gaping hole and a plume of dust. At the same time, a surge of energy came to his mind: the feel of wind and the blur of speed.

Jix hurtled past them, through the hole and into the generator anteroom.

Gevri and Wendomer ran in after her.

Jix already had one soldier pinned on the ground. Through the chalky mist, Gevri targeted the guns and took them apart with dominion. Metal pieces rang and rattled as they bounced on the stone floor. Jix let out a terrifying roar.

Gevri counted five men cowering before Jix. That meant that two of them had gotten into the generator room. The black powder marks around the door to the generator confirmed it. They must have blown open the door while Gevri had been roasting the fat pig.

"Take out this trash, Jix," Gevri said, nodding at the Nau soldiers. "Wendomer, you're with me."

"Yes, sir."

Wendomer didn't have telepathy, which meant she couldn't use dominion to send psychic messages, but she could still receive messages. Gevri explained the plan as they crept toward the generator room. *I need you to find where they've planted the explosives. Once you do, picture it clearly in your head, and hold on to that image no matter what happens. Understand?*

Wendomer nodded. She was conscientious for a girl so young, and Gevri had no doubt she would follow orders.

Now, follow my lead, Gevri added as he slipped through the door.

The first order of business was to get those last two

Nau soldiers out in the open. "I know you're in here!" Gevri called.

As if on cue, two soldiers stepped out from behind a cooling tank about thirty yards ahead. "Stop right there," one of them said, both soldiers aiming their handguns at Gevri and Wendomer.

Gevri raised his hands slowly; Wendomer did the same. But Gevri knew that Wendomer was using clairvoyance to search for the explosives, even with a handgun pointed at her head. She had been trained well.

"Don't move a muscle, or we'll blow the whole place to splinters," the soldier said.

"Okay, now," Gevri said, getting a good look at their guns. Gevri had studied Nau weaponry, but these looked like new models. They were similar to the GS-98, with some extra thing-a-whizzies that Gevri'd never seen before. That was a problem, because if he didn't know exactly what the gun looked like inside, it was hard to take it apart without firing it accidentally. These were the times he wished he had clairvoyance, which would allow him to look inside the guns.

The detonator. If he could find the detonator that the Nau were using to trigger the explosives, he could disable that. But neither of the soldiers seemed to be holding it.

Taking a huge gamble, Gevri took a step forward.

"Watch it!" one of the soldiers yelled, while the other reacted by moving one hand to his hip.

Ah, the detonator is in his pocket.

Gevri needed to see the detonator to determine what type it was. Without that information, he wouldn't be able to disable it. Idiot Nau! Why couldn't he have clipped it to his belt like a normal soldier?

Okay, think, Gevri told himself. He couldn't disable the guns or the detonator. He could grab the guns and fling them out the nearest window, but then the soldier could simply detonate the explosives.

"You two Republikites, step over to that wall," the Nau soldier said. "Good and slow."

Gevri inched sideways. The only way to get out of this mess was to find the explosives themselves, and only Wendomer could do that. *Have you found them?*

Gevri didn't dare look directly at Wendomer, but he caught the tiniest of nods in his peripheral vision.

It was time for the next gamble. If—and this was a big if—*if* Wendomer held a strong enough image in her head,

Gevri would be able to read it. It wouldn't enable him to use telekinesis to move the explosives—he'd still need to see them for himself—but if Wendomer could show him where to look, he just might succeed.

As he took slow backward steps toward the wall, Gevri tried to connect with Wendomer's thoughts. At first, he wasn't getting anything. Then it came to him clear as church chimes: an image of blue explosive putty, two bricks of it, wedged underneath a huge yellow metal box. And if Gevri guessed right, it was the same huge yellow metal box that he and Wendomer were being led toward. It made perfect sense. The soldiers meant to tie them up near the explosives, then run out of the building and trigger the detonator.

Gevri looked over his shoulder under pretense of watching where he was going and spied a corner of the blue putty. That was all he needed to see.

Gently, so gently, he used dominion to loosen the two bricks of putty from under the yellow box, keeping their wirings intact. A few more easy nudges, and Gevri had the explosives floating under the generator toward the soldiers, slowly so that they wouldn't see.

Now the explosive putty, still wired up, hovered behind the soldiers' backs, just over their heads.

Wendomer chuckled softly.

Gevri brought the explosive putty down in front of the soldiers' faces and watched their eyes nearly drop out of their sockets.

"One for you," Gevri said, using dominion to mold one brick of putty around each of the soldiers' guns. "And one for you."

The soldier with the detonator turned to the other with a look of panic, and Gevri spied a corner of the detonator peeking out of his pocket. Just a peek was all Gevri needed. With dominion, he easily slid the device out of the soldier's pocket. Now Gevri held the detonator. One of the soldiers glared and tried to throw his gun down, but Gevri caught it before it hit the floor. "You probably want to be careful with these," he warned.

He sent a message to Jix. *A little help in here?*

Jix came trotting into the room and let loose a rumbling growl. One soldier turned to run, but Jix pounced and slammed him up against the wall. Gevri heard a sick thud but refused to feel sorry for the Nau soldier who, one minute ago, had been planning Gevri's and Wendomer's deaths. Jix paced in front of the remaining soldier as Gevri took a moment to completely disarm the explosives, pull apart the wiring, and disassemble the detonation device. He moved the explosives, now mere blobs of blue putty, to a shelf until the commander could send someone to dispose of them properly. And the guns he handed to Wendomer. "Find the safety latch on these."

Cindahad came running out from behind the generator.

Gevri stepped forward and put his arm around her shoulders. "You okay?"

The girl's shoulders started to shake.

"Everything's okay now," Gevri whispered.

Cindahad broke into a braying laugh. "I saw the whole thing! The looks on their faces!"

"'One for you, and one for you,'" Wendomer said, imitating Gevri's voice. That sent them both into fits of snorting laughter.

And that was enough to make Gevri laugh, too.

Two hours later, the reinforcements from the Republikite army had arrived at Ohandai, and Gevri's strike force was honorably relieved from duty. They had completed their mission with commendation, which put everyone in the mood to celebrate. The whole strike force was in the mess hall, gathered around a huge platter of fried gosta and chits.

Berliott was telling her version of the story. She'd watched Gevri and Wendomer with remote viewing. "And then you know what she said? 'The fat pig is squealing!'"

Another chorus of laughter echoed around the table.

Pik was the only quiet one. He had only recently woken up and heard what had happened. "I missed all the fun."

Gevri gave him a pat on the back. "That was my fault, not yours."

"You owe me some fun, then," Pik said.

"Agreed," said Gevri. "As soon as I have any fun, I'll give it to you."

Laughter rang out again, then stopped abruptly.

"What?" Gevri asked, but when he saw his strike force standing up, each with a stiff palm-outward salute, he knew a superior officer had walked up behind him. That was the trouble with superior officers: they never let anybody relax.

Gevri pushed his chair back, turned to face the officer, and assumed the proper stance. He stiffened that pose even more when he saw his father staring back at him. Why hadn't anyone told him the general was coming?

"General Sarin, sir," Gevri said with a crisp salute.

"Lieutenant Sarin, your strike force is earning quite a reputation," the general said curtly.

"Yes, sir." Gevri wished his father hadn't picked such an undignified moment to show up. "We've just completed a difficult mission, and the soldiers are letting off a little steam. I . . . I didn't realize you would be here, sir."

"I came along with the reinforcements. I wanted to be the one to give you the news." He paused, which was his way of heightening tension, waiting until the whole room would beg for the next word from his mouth if they had the guts to speak in his presence.

Before, when he and his father argued constantly, this would have annoyed the spit out of Gevri, and he would have made some ugly comment to take the wind out of his father's sails. But now Gevri understood his father's need to create a moment. Gevri even played into it, letting the pause have its desired effect before he spoke up. "News? What news?"

"The Archon Special Strike Force has been awarded the Medallion of Honor."

A cheer erupted in the mess hall. Gevri had never felt prouder of his little squadron. They had earned this. Even more important than the medallion were the cheers from the regular troops. Clearly the archons were beginning to gain the respect they deserved.

After a few seconds, General Sarin raised both hands as a signal for quiet. "That's not all. Lieutenant, your strike force has surpassed all expectations. Your training is complete. The Archon Special Strike Force has been officially reassigned to the Kanjai Outpost."

It took a few seconds for Gevri to realize what his father was saying. "You mean—?"

"Yes." The general smiled, which was a rare sight. "It's time to prepare for the attack on Deliverance."

NAU MILITARY INTEL ADMIN LOGBOOK

> Report filed by Military Investigator U. Felmark Puster
[ID# 229-8831-305]. Hypotheses include use of psychic
powers by underage military personnel. Recommend
further information gathering. <

> Additional funding requested. Fund Allocation Request
HVSF10711-37. <

4 TAEMON

"What? What do you want me to see?" Taemon asked.

"I can't tell you. You just have to see it." Amma led him through the streets to a neighborhood close to where he had grown up.

Taemon had to dodge through the crowd to keep up with Amma. Why were so many people on the streets at this hour? It was nearly sunset on a workday, and usually the streets in this neighborhood were fairly quiet.

The crowd grew denser. Amma grabbed his hand and pulled him past the people who were standing around.

When they came to the fountain, he knew what the fuss was about.

Water.

Running water.

For the first time since The Fall, water ran through the city pipes in Deliverance.

Amma stood next to him, watching his reaction.

"I wish you could have seen this fountain before The Fall," Taemon said. "It was a sight to behold. All these streams of water flowing in graceful arcs." Taemon tried to make the motion with his hands. "When I was little, I used to think that the water was jumping and playing a game with its friends."

"It's still beautiful," Amma said. "In a different way. People are learning to do things with their hands. They're starting to accept that psi is gone. This is a big step toward what we've hoped for."

"A very big step." The expressions of pride and awe on the faces in the crowd told him as much.

A long line of people waited for their turn at the spout, carrying all manner of buckets and containers. No bucket in Deliverance had ever had a handle, but now people had added makeshift handles from rope, twine, or twisted fabric. The man at the spout was filling several crystal vases with water, then carefully arranging them in a fabric-lined garbage can that he strapped around his shoulders. The next woman stepped up to the spout with a silver bowl that had a braided rope handle woven through the loopy decorative trim.

The odd mix of old and new, elegant and crude, smooth and rough was inspiring. It represented transition. Change. Acceptance. It was beautiful, as Amma said.

Taemon looked over the line of people waiting. They were laughing and chatting with their neighbors. One woman was explaining to another how she had made her bucket, and when she was done, the other woman explained her own technique. They were sharing ideas, working together, and celebrating success. Small children had taken their shoes off so they could splash and play in the puddles that collected on the floor of the fountain's basin. This never would have been allowed before The Fall. It made his heart swell with hope.

The words of the Heart of the Earth came back to him: *Your work is not finished. You will yet act on behalf of the people of Deliverance.*

A spray of water startled Taemon out of his thoughts.

Amma had bent down over one of the puddles and splashed him.

"You look so serious! This is a happy day." She splashed him again. "Remember the *Sea Flea*? That was fun."

"I remember you made me be the captain," Taemon said. "And I fell in the water."

"You were a good captain," she said. "And you had fun."

"And I had fun." He stomped on a puddle and splashed Amma's legs. She laughed and started to splash him back, but stopped suddenly. Her smile fell as she squinted at something behind Taemon.

"Amma. Taemon. I thought that was you," a timid voice said.

Taemon turned to see a girl with her hair tied back with a string. "Vangie?"

She lowered her head, fidgeting with her hair and looking away. "So many times I thought about coming to find you at the colony. You know, to apologize. I just couldn't quite . . . I don't know."

Taemon had no idea what to say to her. He remembered the awful feeling of betrayal when he learned that Vangie had stolen the sketches in his journal and used them as a bartering tool with Elder Naseph. The next day, Naseph and Yens had come and taken all the books from Amma's family's secret library—books that would make them nearly invincible. But now all of that seemed like ages ago. All the things that had happened since then—the struggle against Naseph and Yens at the temple, The Fall, the trip to Kanjai—all of that seemed necessary somehow. Fated.

But Taemon wasn't sure Amma saw it that way. The loss of those books still weighed heavily on her conscience. He watched Amma's reactions carefully. She stood stiffly, her hands clenched, but he could see no anger in her eyes. Just . . . sadness.

"Did you have any idea?" Amma whispered. "Any idea at all of what you were doing?"

Vangie's eyebrows lifted, and she finally looked Amma in the eye. "No. No. I swear to you, I didn't know they were planning to take the books. I didn't even know what they were looking for. I had talked to Elder Othaniel a few times—my cousin arranged the meetings. Skies, my parents would have died if they knew. All he said was to look for anything unusual. Secret passageways, hidden places, things like that. And that door—when Taemon pointed it out, I started wondering. Then I found those sketches, and I thought finally I would get to go live in the city. I swear, I had no idea . . ." Her words started to sound a little squeaky, and she paused, pressing her lips together to keep from crying. "I'm so sorry."

Amma stepped forward and hugged Vangie. Taemon saw the girl's shoulders shaking.

"It's all right," he heard Amma whisper. "All of us made some bad choices then."

Elder Othaniel. That name was familiar to Taemon. If he remembered right, he was one of the high priests who worked for Elder Naseph. Most of the priests had been lying low since The Fall. They weren't seen in public very much. Rumors were that many of them had left the church and returned to their families.

"What happened after you went to the temple?" Taemon asked.

"It was horrible," Vangie said. "The food was disgusting. And they treated me like a slave. They brought in all those books, and they made us go through them, looking for certain books they wanted."

Amma gasped. "You saw the books? In the temple?"

Vangie nodded. "I was one of the few people who could

read. Did you know hardly anybody in the city can read? So I had to do almost all of it. Skies, there were so many books!"

"Elder Othaniel made you do all this?"

"Yes," Vangie said, her eyes flashing with hatred.

"The books." Amma's eyes were wide, and she was almost breathless. "What happened to the books?"

Vangie frowned and shook her head. "So many strange things happened just before The Fall. They made us work all night sorting through the books. Then Elder Othaniel came in and told us to get a couple of hours of sleep. When we came back, the books were gone. All of them. And no one could find Elder Othaniel, either. Elder Naseph was furious, storming around, blaming everyone. Then the power went out and everybody panicked. I'm telling you, it was like an asylum in there. And that was *before* the earthquake."

"So the books were not in the temple when it was destroyed?" Amma asked.

"I don't see how they could have been," Vangie said. "Naseph had people searching the temple from top to bottom looking for those books. They never found them."

Amma fell silent, her mouth agape. There was only one

person who could have taken the books from Naseph: General Sarin. And Taemon would bet his last lamb that Amma was thinking of a way to get them back.

The leaders of the colony and the city had made a habit of meeting in Hannova's office to discuss problems and coordinate plans. Hannova called it the council, and somewhere along the way, Taemon and Amma had become part of it. Maybe it was their journey over Mount Deliverance last autumn and the fact that they were the only ones who had been to Kanjai. Maybe it was Amma's knack for problem solving or the fact that Taemon had psi. While this wasn't public knowledge, most of the leaders knew it.

Today's meeting began with excited talk about the running water. "And not a moment too soon," Solovar said. "This more than anything will give everyone the feeling that things are getting better."

"People can deal with almost anything when their toilets flush," Amma said.

Solovar laughed. "We're not quite at that point, but we will be in a few more weeks. We're making great progress."

"Indeed we are," Hannova said. "What's next? Does anyone have anything else to report?"

"There's something I'd like to bring up," Taemon said. All eyes turned toward him. "I think we should write a peace proposal to send to Kanjai."

The room fell into complete silence.

"A peace proposal?" Amma's father said. "Do you think they'd even read it?"

"It's a good idea," Da said. "What would the proposal say?"

"I think the first step toward peace is to talk to each other," Taemon said. "We could work out some ground rules, some boundaries, with the goal being to live side by side without fighting."

He looked at the faces in the room—Hannova, Solovar, Challis, Mr. Parvel and Amma, Da, and Drigg. Frowns, mostly, and knitted brows, but an encouraging look from Amma.

"Do you really think they're still going to attack us?" Challis asked. "Seems to me that if that was their plan, they would have done it by now."

"The last thing Gevri said to me was a vow to come back and destroy Deliverance," said Taemon. "I'm pretty sure he meant it."

Hannova leaned forward in her seat. "Yes, but Gevri

is not in charge of the army. He doesn't make all the decisions. Besides, people say unreasonable things when they're angry."

Da spoke up next. "Let's say for the sake of argument that Hannova's right and the Republik has no plans to attack. Wouldn't it still be a good idea to work out an understanding between the two countries?"

Taemon was not sure that the Republik thought of Deliverance as its own country. More like a no-man's-land. But Da's point was a good one.

Drigg scowled. "If we were to write this peace proposal, how would we get it to General Sarin? Someone would have to take it."

"I suppose we could send a runner," Mr. Parvel said. "We know the way to the tunnel by now."

"No," Hannova said. "We have no idea how General Sarin feels toward us right now. We've had absolutely no communication since the attack last winter, and I won't send someone into an unknown situation like that."

Taemon's heart leaped. He wasn't even sure if anyone would go for the peace proposal idea, and now it seemed they might actually do it.

"I'll take care of that," Taemon said.

Hannova wagged her finger at Taemon. "Oh, no. You're not going to Kanjai again so soon. Not until we know more about the situation. You barely got back alive last time."

"That's not what I meant. I'm not planning on going there—I promise. I have an idea." It would mean using psi, but he didn't mention that. He still felt uncomfortable talking about his psi to others—though they probably guessed that's what he meant.

"I suppose it can't hurt," Solovar said. "It's either that or do nothing and hope for the best."

After the meeting, Amma's father had stayed to talk to Solovar, and Taemon walked Amma home.

"I think the peace proposal is a great idea," Amma said. "Is that what you came up with when you were up on the mountain?"

"Cha, sort of." It was his own answer to what the Heart of the Earth had asked of him, but that seemed too complicated to explain.

"Well, it's brilliant." Her words brought a warmth to the back of his neck. He wondered if it showed.

Amma kept talking. "If we can just talk to General

Sarin, and maybe Gevri, too. If we can just sit down and work things out, I'm sure there's some way to . . ."

Amma trailed off. They were almost at her house now, the one that had been rebuilt after Yens and Naseph had destroyed her family's home that hid the secret library. Amma ran ahead and picked up something that lay next to the door. "What's this?"

Taemon hurried to catch up. Amma held an unusual package. It was wrapped in colorful flowered fabric, perhaps a scrap from an old tablecloth, with a piece of twine wound around the package diagonally. Into the twine, little sprigs of wildflowers had been tucked and arranged carefully.

"I think it's from Vangie," Amma whispered.

It made sense. Vangie's birth sign was Flower, and she did everything with an artistic flair.

Amma turned the package over and pulled out a note tucked in the twine. She had it open in a blink. Taemon read over her shoulder.

Dear Amma,
I kept this book because Elder Othaniel told us to look
for books about how Nathan discovered psi. I thought

if I had something he wanted, I could bargain for better food and more free time.

Now I'm giving it to you as a way to say I'm sorry. What I did was wrong. I know that now. I hope somehow we can still be friends.

Vangie

She had drawn a flower with a stem that looped around her name.

Amma let the fabric and the twine fall to her feet. She now held an ancient leather-bound book. "*The Mind That Unlocked Psi*, by Kertrand Lasky," she read from the spine. "What in the Great Green Earth?"

"Have you ever seen that book before?" Taemon asked.

"Not that I remember. Maybe my da will recognize it." She hugged the book to her chest. "Someday I hope we'll get all the books back from the Republik. I'd like to think this is a start. My family was charged with preserving the history of Deliverance. I still need to carry that out as best I can."

"I'd like to help," Taemon said.

"Thanks." She beamed at him, which made his neck heat up again; then she ran into the house with the book.

Taemon walked home, wondering who Kertrand Lasky was and why Elder Othaniel had been so interested in books about Nathaniel.

Taemon sat alone in his room in Drigg's house, staring at the peace proposal in his hand. It had been a week since the meeting, and everyone seemed to warm up to the idea of a peace negotiation. Hannova had proposed it to the council, and they had given their approval. Now it was up to him to get this message to General Sarin.

He stared at the words and repeated the message to himself until he had it memorized.

Representatives of the people of Deliverance respectfully request a meeting with the people of the Republik to discuss ways in which our two societies can live side by side in peace, without fear of oppression or war.

One sentence. He'd made them trim it down to one sentence; it was the most he thought he could send. That had caused a lot of argument, but Taemon insisted that details could be worked out later. This was just the first gesture.

Taemon let out a big breath. Time to get to work.

Using clairvoyance, he began sending his awareness along the route that led to the tunnel, through the mountain, into Kanjai. He stretched his psionic senses as far as he could. But the farther he went, the dimmer his awareness felt. He broke the connection. That wasn't the answer.

Time to try something new. He'd been to Kanjai. He knew the building where General Sarin trained the archons. If he could imagine that place, recall it in his mind in great detail, maybe he could send his awareness directly there instead of trying to stretch it out over a long distance.

It took him a few minutes to fully create the scene in his mind. He found it was easier if he focused on one small part of the building. He picked one wall in the building that he had walked past many times during the time he spent in Kanjai, the wall between his cell and the training gym.

He pictured it clearly, in every detail, just as he would if he were trying to use psi to move it. He gathered psi and tried to make a connection with the wall . . . and there! The connection was made.

Next he pictured the words of the peace proposal written into the paint on the wall. He told himself this wouldn't be that hard, that it was just like changing the colors of the holes when he used to play psiball. All he had to do was picture the words on the wall and change the color of the gray paint to . . . blue. That was his old psiball team color. He pictured the letters in neat, tidy handwriting, so it wouldn't look too much like vandalism. He wasn't trying to deface property; he just wanted to get the message to the general. He was just going to paint the words on the wall.

He imagined the gray wall with the blue words on it. Held it in his mind. Every i dotted and every t crossed. When he had it clearly in his mind, he gave the order. *Be it so!*

And the words were there. He couldn't say exactly how he knew it had worked, but he was certain it had.

Now what?

How soon would General Sarin respond? And how would he send his reply? The Republik used their strange-fangled devices, radios and phones, to send messages. But of course there were no radios and phones in Deliverance. Not even in the days of psi. Those kinds of things had never appealed to psi wielders, who distrusted mechanical devices, especially those designed to transmit information.

Taemon took a deep breath. They would just have to wait and see how Sarin chose to respond. For now, he should probably report back to Hannova and tell her that the message had been sent. He slipped out the back door of Drigg's workshop and into the afternoon heat, heading toward Hannova's place. He took all of three steps before he stopped cold.

A message. Gouged into the stucco of the back wall of Drigg's house. Not neat little words printed onto the wall, but deep, slashing letters scored into the plaster:

We will discuss the proposal. Meet us inside the tunnel in three days.

The quickness of the response wasn't the only thing that disturbed Taemon. Whoever had used dominion to carve those letters had to have seen Drigg's house, which meant that General Sarin's spies hadn't been restricted to the temple.

NAU MILITARY INTEL ADMIN LOGBOOK

.· Report of Findings filed by Board of Inquiry re: Matter
8-047a through 8-047j. Summary: Hypotheses suggested
by Military Investigator U. Felmark Puster [TD# 229-8831-
305] are unreasonable. Board requests more aggressive
information-gathering techniques. <

> Additional funding approved. Reference: Allocation
Document HVSF10711-45. <

5 GEVRI

The transport vehicle jostled and bounced the young
archons along the endless road. Gevri watched the billow-
ing dust the tires stirred up, glad it wasn't his job to drive.
On a flat, featureless road like this, surrounded by eternal
fields of wheat stubble, driving was the most boring job
he could think of. Two soldiers sat in the front seats: one
off duty and dozing, the other at the wheel.

Three days of land travel would get them back to
Kanjai, where they would stage the attack on Nathan's
people. In the old times, the army would have used planes

to transport soldiers, but the Nau had dominated the airspace for some time now, and the army allowed only fighter planes in the air. All troop movements were safer by ground. In this case, Gevri had mixed feelings.

The bad part was that Jix refused to travel with them. To her, a vehicle was just another cage, and she would have none of it. She knew how to get back to Kanjai, and she preferred to travel on foot and on her own. Being separated from her for that long made him uneasy, but there was no arguing with a jaguar.

The upside to three days of driving was the time it gave Gevri to get his team in the right state of mind, which was crucial. He sensed that his archons were reluctant about the attack on Deliverance, and that had to be dealt with. "Great leaders are comfortable with conflict," his father always said, "not because we enjoy it, but because we are eager to get beyond it." And that is exactly what Gevri needed to do right now. Face the conflict head-on so he could get beyond it.

"Listen," Gevri said. "I think I know what's bothering you about the next mission. You likely heard about some of the tricks the Nathanites pulled on us when we attempted to attack their city. Let's get one thing straight:

they do not have dominion, or 'psi.' They used tricks to fool us, to frighten us. But that's not going to happen again."

"How can you be sure they don't have psi?" said Saunch.

"Yens still has powers," Wendomer added. "They say he's the True Son."

Gevri grimaced and ran his fingers over his stubbly hair. "First of all, the person who came to Kanjai and pretended to be Yens is not the True Son. His name is Taemon. He lied to you about who he was. He lied to us all.

"Second, there is no such thing as a True Son. All of that is taken from old legends—legends that no one in the Republik believes anymore. It's another trick, don't you see? A trick to make people afraid. We're not falling for it."

Gevri paused, wishing they would meet his gaze. Some looked at their feet; some looked out the back of the vehicle. Gevri continued anyway. "Let me tell you what really happened. This Nathanite named Taemon came to the Republik. I know at least some of you met him while he was here, but I spent a lot of time with him. I went to Deliverance. I was there for most of a day. I know the truth. Taemon is the only one with any power. And remember, their power is not exactly like dominion. They call it psi, and it works a little differently. When archons exercise dominion, they use their hands and their voices as outward signs of the invisible power they are using. Let me tell you, psi doesn't work that way. It's sneaky. No hand movements. No voice signals. You can't tell who is doing what. That makes it easy to fake."

Saunch nodded slowly. "I remember Yens—I mean Taemon—talking about hand movements. He said they weren't necessary."

Gevri paused. Taemon had spent only three days in the archon facility, but it was impossible to know how much of his poison had infected them. "Believe me when I tell you," Gevri continued, "that Taemon was just as sneaky as all of the Nathanites. He came to spy on us. Not to make friends, not to help, not to teach. He came to find out what our army was all about so the Nathanites could beat us when the time came. Now he's going to find out what we're really capable of."

He paused again, this time to let the truth sink in.

Neeza raised her head and looked timidly at Gevri. "I thought he came to look for his da."

"Where did you hear that?" Gevri heard his words coming fast and loud. He took a deep breath. He needed to remove emotions from the equation and use logic and reasoning. "The prisoner he said he was looking for wasn't his da at all. This whole thing was a scheme for gathering information about the Republik."

Neeza looked down again and hunched her shoulders.

He took a breath and again willed himself to speak calmly. "The Nathanites are the enemy, just as much as the Nau are."

"But—" Neeza began.

"They're not the same as the Nau," Berliott blurted out.

Pik nodded. "After all, they used to be Republikites."

"Exactly," Gevri said. "They're traitors. They turned their backs on the Republik. That makes them worse."

"But can't we just talk to them?" Neeza said. "Do we really have to go to war against them?"

The look on her face tugged at Gevri's heart. She should be home, playing fox-and-goose and begging for one more samkin. But ever since General Sarin had selected her for training, the army was the closest thing to her home, and the archons were the closest thing to her family. Gevri tried to speak as gently as he could manage.

"Talking things out with liars doesn't work, Neeza. You can't believe anything they say. Promises and agreements mean nothing to them."

A bump in the road gave them a jolt, and everyone had to shift back into a comfortable position. Gevri paused and searched the young faces of his unit. Did they trust him? Were they united? "My father's plan is the only way. We have to eliminate this threat, or they will team up with the Nau. Just think, if the Nau—"

The hum of the tires changed its pitch. They were slowing down. "Hold on a second."

Gevri unbuckled his seat belt and stepped into the cab. He kept his voice low. "What's wrong?"

"Nothing to worry about," the driver answered. "Tire puncture. Have to slow down to fifty, but we can drive another two hundred miles before we have to change it. We'll reach Fort Limner long before that."

"Can you tell what caused it?"

"Negative, sir. Could've been anything."

"Which means it could be deliberate. Stay alert, soldier."

"Yes, sir," the driver said, nudging his companion awake.

Gevri settled back into his seat with an uneasy feeling. Had the Nau caused the tire puncture? Were they trying to slow the convoy? If they wanted to attack the convoy, they would do it in a straight-up surprise attack: grenade launchers, high-speed rifles, the works. Slowing them down first wouldn't be necessary. Still, his instincts were telling him that this was no coincidence.

"Pik, have you been studying that Nau handbook of military devices?"

The boy nodded. "Every night, sir."

"Have you gotten to the tire-puncture devices? Can you remember what they look like?"

"Yes, sir. I think so."

"I want you to use remote viewing and cast your sight on the road behind us. Go as far back as you can. Any puncture devices back there?"

"I'll check, sir." Pik turned and stared through the small window in the back door.

"Cindahad and Berliott, I want you two to use remote viewing to look ahead. Look for anything suspicious, anything that seems unnatural, anything at all."

"Yes, sir."

"Anything we can do, sir?" Saunch asked.

"No," Gevri answered. "Until we know what we're dealing with, we'll just have to—"

"Sir," Berliott blurted out. "I see something! It looks like—"

"Gas!" the driver yelled. Brakes squealed as whiteness billowed around the windows.

"Don't stop!" Gevri yelled. "Our best chance is to drive through the cloud."

The vehicle jolted forward. "I can't see anything, sir!" the driver cried.

"Working on it!" Gevri called on dominion and tried to move the gas away from the front of the vehicle. Gods! Gas was the hardest thing to move with dominion. So dispersed. So flimsy. Nothing to push against. And being inside a moving vehicle didn't help. They moved through the gas quicker than he could make a connection with it. He created a bubble of clear air traveling along with them, just in front of the windshield. He tried to expand that bubble, but the biggest he could make it was only a few feet.

"Still can't see, sir!" the driver said, his voice tense.

The transport vehicle bounced crazily, which meant they were no longer on the road. Fortunately, they were surrounded by a field of wheat stubble and so weren't in danger of crashing. But all the bouncing made it hard to keep the bubble next to the windshield.

"It's no use!" Cindahad shouted. "The gas cloud is huge."

"And it's getting bigger," Berliott added. "They've planted canisters all over. Someone is activating them remotely."

How could they fight this? Gevri inventoried all the different ways the archons could use dominion, but nothing seemed helpful for the situation. Remote viewing told them what they were up against, but nothing more. Telekinesis was useless when you couldn't see the thing you were trying to move. He couldn't think of a way to use psychometry or retrocognition in this scenario.

Thwak. Thwak. Thwak. Something was striking the armored transportation vehicle. "Cindahad, what's hitting us?"

"Bullets, sir. From above."

"Saunch, get the gas masks!" Gevri yelled, and Saunch immediately unbuckled and lurched to the equipment bin. If those bullets pierced the hull of the vehicle, the gas would creep in and disable them. He didn't know what kind of gas this was, or what effect it had, and he didn't want to find out.

"How are they shooting at us?" Gevri asked. "Helicopter?"

"No, sir, no helicopter," Pik said. "Paratroopers are drifting toward us and shooting. I count nine of them."

Thwak. Thwak. By now, everyone had on gas masks, including both soldiers.

Gevri took a deep breath through his mask. This was some kind of big operation. *Calm down. Calm down and think clearly. How can the paratroopers aim in this fog?*

Gevri hadn't realized it, but he had linked telepathically with Saunch, because the boy's voice came clearly into Gevri's mind: *They must be able to see the movement. Where the fog swirls, that's where we are.*

Gevri thumbed the radio switch on his gas mask. "Driver, stop the vehicle and kill the engine."

"Yes, sir."

"Berliott, let me know when all the paratroopers are on the ground."

"Not quite yet, sir. Two more."

Thwak. Thwak. Thwak.

Hissssss.

"They're coming for us, sir," the soldier in the passenger seat said.

"Good." Gevri's voice echoed in his own ears. "When they get close enough, we'll have the advantage." The truth was, he could not think of any advantage when the paratroopers closed in, but it sounded good. Had Saunch's sensitive telepathic ability allowed him to pick up on that thought? If it did, his face didn't show it.

"Everyone stay inside," Gevri said. "There's no reason for anyone to go with me."

"But sir—" Saunch began, but Gevri cut him off.

"No reason. What you need to do you can do from inside the vehicle. What I need to do I can only do outside. Keep your gas masks secure and your radios open, everyone. Communication. Unity." He looked at each pair of eyes staring at him through the visors on their gas masks. "We can get through this."

As he eased the door open, white tendrils of gas seeped inside. Gevri slid into the milky fog, closed the door softly, and crept to the front of the vehicle. "I need my remote viewers to find those paratroopers and tell me where they are," Gevri instructed through his radio. "I need direction and I need distance. The front of the vehicle is twelve o'clock. Talk to me."

Cindahad was the first to respond. "Two paratroopers at one o'clock. Approximately two hundred sixty yards."

Gevri called on dominion and began to clear the fog away so that he had a clear line of sight. He had to be quick. Once the path was cleared, they would be able to shoot without any trouble. He had to get to their guns before they could react.

He cleared his mind and focused on where he expected those two paratroopers to be. He cleared a little more fog, a little more . . . and there! In an instant, Gevri flung their rifles deep into the fog. Gods, they had sidearms, too! Those, too, disappeared into the fog before the soldiers could fire. The two paratroopers recovered quickly from the surprise and began charging toward Gevri. Predictable. This part was easy enough. Gevri removed their gas masks and sent those into the fog as well. The two Nau soldiers took only a couple more steps, then fell to the ground. Were they dead? Or just unconscious? Gevri did not care to find out.

"Got them," he radioed back to the other archons. "Find me another. Give me the closest one first."

This time, Pik answered. "One paratrooper at ten o'clock, one hundred twenty-five yards."

Gevri disabled the next paratrooper in the same way. Now he knew to get rid of the sidearm and the rifle at the same time. Both guns went flying behind the soldier into the fog, followed by the gas mask.

"One paratrooper at six o'clock, one hundred yards."

"Two at three o'clock, one hundred fifty yards."

Gevri took care of the three soldiers handily. The fog swirled back over their motionless bodies. Six soldiers had been immobilized. Three more to go.

"Where's the next one?" Gevri asked over the radio.

"One paratrooper at eight o'clock, two hundred yards," Berliott said.

Again, Gevri used dominion to sweep the fog away, clearing a path toward his attacker. "Where is he?" Gevri whispered. "I can't see him."

"He's moving," Berliott said. "Counterclockwise. To your left."

Cautiously, Gevri widened the clearing. Still no sign of the paratrooper.

Like a ghost, the Nau paratrooper stepped out of the mist, firing his rifle. Gevri had no time to call on dominion, but he did manage to duck. The bullet glanced off the clasp of his gas mask.

Gevri gasped with relief and wasted no time getting rid of the soldier's guns. "Got him," he radioed back. "Two more. Find them for me."

"Two at five o'clock, two hundred twenty-five yards."

That's when his eyes began to sting. He checked his gas mask. The seal was loose. He smelled a sour odor. Like pickles. He tried to fix the seal, but his hands felt numb. And the buckle was busted. That bullet must have hit it. Gods, he hated pickles.

"Sir?" Gevri heard over the radio. "They're coming in fast. Five o'clock. One hundred yards."

"I'll take care of them," Gevri said, dropping to his knees. He had to hold on long enough to get rid of the guns. Two black shapes appeared against the white fog. But everything was blurry. He couldn't see the guns.

The blackness around the edges of his vision grew, then the world vanished into a blinding white, and Gevri collapsed.

6 TAEMON

Taemon didn't have to tell Hannova about the message scratched on the wall, because word of mouth beat him to it. Before the sun had set, Taemon found himself in another council meeting at Hannova's office to discuss this latest development. Why did adults always insist on meetings? It made him feel like he was in trouble.

Then again, he *was* in trouble, along with all of Deliverance.

"Three days?" said Drigg. "The delegation will have to

leave tomorrow to get there in time. That's no easy trip, even in the summertime."

"How many people are we talking about?" Solovar asked.

"This whole thing is just too risky," interrupted Mr. Parvel. "I can't guarantee the safety of the delegation."

Of course not, Taemon thought. *No one can guarantee anyone's safety.* But he kept quiet. It was just their fear talking right now. They needed some time to get over the shock of it all.

"Everybody settle down," Hannova said. "Let's work on one thing at a time. I've already got people working on gathering provisions for the trip. But we need to decide who's going."

When it was all hammered out, seven people had been named to the delegation. Hannova would represent the colony, and Solovar would represent the city. Da was going to represent Free Will and its followers. Amma's father and her two adult brothers would be bodyguards for the group. And Taemon would go because he was the one General Sarin had invited—and, he suspected, because he had psi. He couldn't blame them for feeling safer with a psi wielder around, even if he himself wasn't ever quite sure how best to help out.

Drigg would drive them as far as he could in the hauler; they'd have to walk the rest of the way. Amma had argued to be included, but her father refused to allow it.

They were trying to settle on a departure time when Yens burst into the room.

"I demand to be part of this council. I'm the True Son. I'm the one General Sarin should be negotiating with."

"Sit down, Yens," Da said.

"I'm an influential leader in the city," Yens continued. "I should be included in this. I should—"

"Then sit down like your da told you." Hannova stared Yens down until he sat in the seat between Solovar and Mr. Parvel, who jumped to his feet.

"Do I need to remind everyone that this is the maniac who burned my home and stole the books from the library? That one act began all of this! I don't care who he thinks he is. He doesn't belong here!"

"He assaulted me, too, Birch," Hannova said. "But many unhappy events led to The Fall. I'm not convinced they were all Yens's doing."

"That's right," said Yens. "It was Naseph. He had this whole scheme worked out with General Sarin, and he only told me parts of it. He told me we needed the library to keep the Republik in check, but I had no idea that he would destroy your home to get at the library."

Amma's father stood up with clenched fists. He glared at Yens and took a deep breath through flared nostrils. Taemon winced, anticipating the shouting that was sure to follow, but it was Amma who spoke next.

"But the books ended up in the Republik," Amma said. She spoke forcefully but calmly. "Would you care to explain that?"

"There were spies from the Republik in the temple. Not even Naseph knew that until it was too late." Yens's tone was careless, as though he fully expected them to believe him and to grant him a spot on the delegation. His talents for using charisma and confidence to get what he wanted had started when he was captain of his psiball team, and he'd sharpened them in the past couple of years at the temple.

"It doesn't matter," Da said. "Naseph was a self-serving, weak leader, and everyone knows that now. He doesn't even come out of the temple anymore, from what I hear.

The priests from the temple take shifts at the farms and queue up at the food lines just like everyone else these days."

Solovar nodded. "The church isn't supported by the people anymore, and not just because they can't afford it. I'd say that many people feel that church isn't even relevant anymore. The church existed to regulate psi, and that's gone now."

"Now, just one minute," Da interrupted. "The church was never about psi. The church was there to help people turn their hearts to the Heart of the Earth. That hasn't changed—psi or no psi."

Solovar shrugged. "I'm just explaining the general sentiment in the city."

"This is where I come in," Yens said. "As the True Son, I can be the leader that people turn to for spiritual guidance. I can bring the church's influence back to the people."

"I'm not sure that will work," Solovar said. "Some people think the True Son thing is over and done with. Some people think your psi is gone now, too."

Yens leaned back in his chair and let out an exasperated sigh. "What about the battle with the archons? How do they explain all the things I did to defeat Gevri and his soldiers?"

You mean all the things I did, Taemon thought. But he had made an agreement with Yens to make his brother look like the one with the psi, and he wouldn't go back on that now.

Solovar rubbed the white stubble on his chin. "You haven't displayed your 'powers' since that day. Many people wonder if that was your last act as True Son, if that battle sapped whatever psi you had left."

Yens threw a fierce glare at Taemon.

"Those rumors didn't come from me," Taemon said. "I've kept up my end of the bargain." The truth was, he was happy to let Yens be the public figure of the True Son. Yens was better suited for grand speeches and showy displays. That had never been Taemon's style. "Look, we really don't have time for this right now," Taemon continued. "Let's just figure out what we need to do to make this delegation work."

"He's right," Hannova said. "The rest will have to wait."

"Only if I'm in the delegation," Yens said.

"Fine," said Hannova. She held up a hand to silence

Mr. Parvel's protests. "There will be plenty of people to keep an eye on him, Birch," Hannova assured him. "We won't let him do anything foolish."

Yens smartly kept his mouth shut at this, though Taemon could practically feel his brother bristling. What did he expect, though? Unlike the poor, deluded souls at the temple, everyone in this room knew Yens was a phony and a traitor.

When the meeting was finally over, it was dark. Amma wanted to study the message that had been left by the Republik, so she and Taemon walked back to Drigg's workshop.

"I've been reading the book Vangie gave me," Amma said.

"The one about Kertrand Lasky?"

"Not about him, but written by him. It's slow reading. Really dense, academic stuff. He studied a lot of philosophers of his time. He tried to connect those philosophies to psi and how it worked from a scientific point of view."

"Wait—when was his time?" Taemon asked.

"He lived at the same time Nathan did. He was one

of the original followers who came with Nathan to Deliverance. He was pretty old at the time; he lived most of his life in the Republik."

Taemon thought about that for a moment. "Do you think he saw Mount Deliverance being raised up by Nathan?"

"I haven't read anything about that, but I suppose it's possible. Wouldn't that be incredible?"

Taemon nodded.

"If you want, I'll lend you the book when I'm done," Amma offered.

"Sure, thanks," he said.

They stopped when they came to the wall with the message on it. "The letters look angry and threatening," Amma said. "Do you think they meant it to look that way?"

Taemon shrugged.

"Skies, I can't believe they're letting Yens go and not me."

"Your da just worries about you," Taemon said.

Amma humphed. "He thinks everything's too dangerous. I *need* to go to Kanjai to find out more about the books. Those books rightly belong to the colony. They're part of our history. Not just for the colony, but for all of Deliverance."

"You should talk to your da about it. Maybe you can persuade him to bring it up as part of the negotiations."

Amma frowned. "How would I know that he'd keep his word, though? What if the negotiations don't go well and he decides it's better not to push too hard?" She shook her head. "It has to be me. It's my fault the books were stolen in the first place. I'm the one who needs to get them back—however much it ruffles General Sarin's feathers."

Taemon knew better than anyone just how relentless Amma could be when she set her mind to something. "So how are you going to convince your da to let you come along?"

"Would you come with me when I talk to him?"

"I'm not sure how that'll help. He doesn't like me, remember?"

"That's not true," Amma said, though they both knew her da still placed some of the blame on Taemon for what had happened with the library. "Anyway, with you in the room, he can't yell so much."

"I can think of plenty of times when he's yelled with me in the room."

"It's worth a try. Please?"

Her eyes told him how badly she wanted to go. And he *had* told her he would help. "All right," he said.

Suddenly Amma gasped. She took his arm and turned him around. "Look," she whispered, pointing at the trees near Drigg's house.

Taemon squinted at a silhouette. But of what? Not a person. It looked more like a . . . like a *jaguar.*

"Is that Jix?" Taemon whispered.

Amma nodded. "What's she doing here?"

They watched as the jaguar stood, still as a statue, and stared intently at them.

Taemon felt a shudder run down his spine. That cat always made him nervous, and her stare was thoroughly bone-chilling.

"What's the matter, Jix?" Amma asked gently. "Are you hurt? Is Gevri hurt?"

Jix didn't move a muscle. She stood frozen in place, her eyes fixed on them.

Out of nowhere, strange images and sensations flooded Taemon's mind. He had experienced this once before, but it was no less disconcerting now. Jix had created a telepathic link and was trying to tell him something. The jaguar's thoughts were not expressed in a language, and it was difficult to make sense of them. But she seemed to be showing him a memory.

Jix was in a cage. A cold cement cell with no windows. The floor was damp and smelled of stale urine and putrid meat. Taemon nearly retched from the strong odors. Not only that, but he felt what Jix felt. Sick, weak, hurting all over, and a headache that pounded on her skull. She could barely hold her head up.

Taemon saw gruesome flashes of what had brought her to this state. Experiments. Torture. Withholding food, water, and fresh air. Forcing her to do things she didn't understand and had no desire to do. Forcing her to fight people, hurt people, even kill people. The only way to survive was to do what they wanted—to develop a telepathic ability so she could understand her master's orders and carry them out. The experiment had killed her mate, and it had nearly killed her.

Then Taemon saw Gevri enter the cage. He had long hair, like when Taemon had first met him, and looked quite a bit younger, maybe twelve or so. Jix felt no fear of humans any longer. If this human killed her, she would welcome it. If this human hurt her, it would be but one more drop in a lake of hurt.

The young Gevri approached Jix and did nothing. Said nothing. Only lay next to her on the filthy floor and draped his arm around her. Jix used her telepathic ability to search Gevri's mind for his intentions. She found no malice, but nor did she find pity. Only a desire for companionship.

Every night, young Gevri came to Jix's cage and curled up next to her. Sometimes he brought fresh meat and sweet water. Never before had a human given her good food. In return, Jix taught Gevri how to communicate with telepathy. And one night, when Jix was strong enough, Gevri helped her escape.

Escape. Escape. That part of the message repeated over and over in Taemon's mind. Torture, misery, hopelessness . . . then escape! Alone, helpless. The rescuer comes, and escape! Escape!

Okay, I get that, Taemon tried to relay to Jix. *I understand why you are loyal to Gevri. But why are you telling me this? What does it have to do with me?*

The escape scene from the cement cell vanished.

The connection was still strong, but Jix was pausing. Demanding Taemon's attention but not communicating anything.

What do you want me to do? Taemon asked.

Still nothing, but Jix would not allow Taemon to break the telepathic connection. How did she do that? Jix was one of the strongest telepaths he'd ever experienced.

The images of captivity followed by rescue were repeated over and over, increasing in speed and intensity until it became almost painful.

The connection broke abruptly, and Taemon watched as Jix turned and padded away.

Amma gasped softly. "Did you see that? Jix locked in a cell and Gevri helping her?" Her voice quivered.

"I saw it," Taemon said. "Is that the first time Jix has sent you a message?"

"Yes! But . . . how? I don't have psi."

"You don't have to have psi to receive a message. Only to send one."

"That is the eeriest thing ever." Amma shook her head and let out a big huff. "What was it supposed to mean?"

"I wish I knew," Taemon answered.

NAU MILITARY INTEL ADMIN LOGBOOK

> Activity Report filed by Military Investigator
U. Felmark Puster [ID# 229-8831-305]. Summary: Sleep
deprivation found to be effective in counteracting
abnormal abilities in Republikite prisoners. Interviews
in progress. <

7 GEVRI

How long had it been since he'd slept? Sleep itself seemed like a dream, a thing he used to do in another life, a luxury of days long past. Now he lived in a fog of pain and confusion. A foggy confusion of pain. A confogging fusion of pain.

Fog.

White fog.

Swirling over the brittle stubs of a wheat field.

Where? Where were the soldiers who wanted to shoot him?

Where were the archons? He had to find them. He had to protect them.

Out of the swirling fog stepped Taemon. He held a gun. A bullet hurtled toward Gevri's face. It moved slowly. There was plenty of time to move out of the way. If only he could move. But the fog. The fog was like snow clinging to his legs and freezing him in place. *Can't move. So tired.*

The bullet struck Gevri's gas mask and he flinched.

Pain. Pain shooting through his shoulders.

Then he remembered. He was chained to a chair. His arms were tightly bound behind him. If he let his head drop, the pain was unbearable.

He lifted his head. Tried to balance his head perfectly on his neck so he could relax his muscles a little. There. One tick above unbearable.

His mind drifted into the fog again.

There was something urgent he must do. What was it? He searched his brain. Everything was jumbled. Something to do with the archons . . .

"They depend on you," his father's voice whispered through the fog. "The responsibility falls on you."

"I'll take care of them," Gevri answered. Had he spoken aloud? Was that croaking sound his own voice?

"Gevri? Can you hear me?" said his father. But his voice was also strange. Higher. More nasal. "Are you ready to resume our discussion?"

Gevri opened his eyes. The voice was not his father's. A Nau soldier sat in the chair across from him. Fancy uniform. Dark maroon. Shiny buttons. Blue-black stripe on the sleeve.

That stripe, it meant something. He used to know. Couldn't remember.

"Begin recording," said the soldier. "Military Inspector U. Felmark Puster interrogating prisoner number six-naught-nine-dash-one-one-naught. Let it be noted that the prisoner has been forced to stay awake for five days and three hours. All indications are that he is unable to use any variety of psychic ability. The prisoner will now state his name."

Gevri grunted.

"Let it be noted that the prisoner refuses to identify himself," said Inspector Puster. "First question: By what means were you able to disarm the Nau soldiers?"

Questions. More questions. How many times had the inspector questioned him? Gevri had lost count. Or lost the ability to count. He sighed. It made his shoulders hurt again.

He could answer with one word: dominion. But they were all counting on him. His father, the archons, the whole military. His father had developed dominion as a secret weapon. Finally the Republik had an advantage that would win them independence from the Nau for good. Only a weak, ugsome coward would give in to this torture and tell them what they wanted to know. He kept silent.

"Let it be noted that the prisoner is uncooperative," said the inspector.

Strobe lights splattered across the floor, the walls, everywhere. Colors, blinding white spots, rotating around the room, then reversing, then spinning again. Gevri scrunched his eyes tight, but the lights were impossible to block out completely.

"Question number two: Where does this ability come from?"

They're counting on me. Ending the war is more important than a few minutes of torture. A distant part of his brain tried to remind him that it had been days, not minutes, but he told himself to shut up.

"Revised question number two: How is this power wielded? That is, what triggers it?"

Gevri imagined himself as a statue cut out of stone. He could not see. He could not hear. He could not speak. He could not feel. He was nothing.

"Turn off the strobe lights," said the inspector. "Perhaps the sleep deprivation is preventing you from forming coherent thoughts. Perhaps I should recommend a short nap. Fifteen minutes, shall we say? If you answer one question, just one, you may sleep for fifteen minutes."

Fifteen minutes of sleep! Paradise!

No. He did not need sleep. He was nothing.

"Let me make this a bit easier for you," the inspector said. "I will tell you what we have already learned from your young friends, the underage soldiers that were captured at the same time you were."

Gevri's stomach clenched. This was the first time the inspector had mentioned the other archons. "My unit? Where are they? What have you done to them? If you hurt them, I swear to you, I will—" He struggled against the cords that bound his wrists. The pain nearly ripped his spine from his flesh, but this time he welcomed it. He deserved it. He was a failure.

U. Felmark Puster laughed. "Oh, my. Let the record show a strong emotional response. Your friends are very near, I assure you. Would you care to visit them? I can authorize that, but only if you cooperate. Now, we are aware that this aberrant ability takes different forms. Here is question three: How many forms of the ability known as dominion are there? Please explain each of its forms in detail."

And Gevri did. Gods save his grimy soul, he answered question three. And question four. And five through eighteen.

He never did get to visit the archons, but he was allowed to sleep for fifteen minutes.

Paradise, just as he'd imagined.

NAU MILITARY INTEL ADMIN LOGBOOK

> Activity Report filed by Military Investigator
U. Felmark Puster [ID# 229-8831-305]. Summary: After
increasing the intensity of interrogation techniques,
the questioning of Republik personnel yielded key
information. The Republikite army is now known to
have 10 units of soldiers with telekinetic abilities.
Additionally, one smaller unit consists of soldiers
with other psychic abilities, namely telepathy,
remote viewing, clairvoyance, psychometry, and
retrocognition. <

> Request for Further Information filed by the Board
of Inquiry. <

8 TAEMON

Taemon sat in the living room of Amma's new house. She'd given him the most comfortable seat in the room, a low-slung chair with leather straps woven together to make the seat and a soft cushion on top of that. But he had never felt more uncomfortable. Amma was explaining to her da why she should be allowed to join the delegation. Mr. Parvel didn't seem to be listening.

"What can I do, Da? What can I do to prove to you that I can do this? I went back to the city with Taemon to confront Naseph. I've traveled across the mountain to Kanjai. I helped Taemon during the battle with the archons. . . ."

"I couldn't have done any of that without her," Taemon added.

Mr. Parvel glared at him.

"Doesn't that prove that I can handle myself? That I'm capable?"

"You also revealed the location of the library," Mr. Parvel said, "which led to the loss of every single book—"

Taemon raised one finger. "Actually, sir, that was me." No one listened.

Mr. Parvel continued his rant. "You left home without permission to go traipsing over the mountain. That doesn't spell out 'responsible' to me."

"Traipsing?" Amma sputtered. "We were trying to save Taemon's da! He would have done the same for me if it had been you captured by the Republik."

Taemon nodded emphatically, but Mr. Parvel wasn't even looking at him.

A pause hung in the room between daughter and father.

"Please, Da," Amma whispered. "I need to go to Kanjai to find a way to bring home the books. I've brought one back already, and I swear to you I will hunt down the others."

Mr. Parvel shook his head sadly. "What do we have to bargain with, Amma? How are we going to ask about books? We'll be lucky enough if we leave the meeting unscathed; the very best we can hope for is a tremulous peace agreement. There's no place for further demands."

Taemon would never admit it, but Mr. Parvel had a point. What could they offer to trade for the books? Somehow Taemon didn't think a simple "please" would do the trick.

But this didn't seem to bother Amma. "I don't know what will happen, Da. But neither do you. None of us knows because none of us has ever been in this situation before. What I do know is that I can't just sit here in Deliverance when there's even the slightest breath of a chance that my going to Kanjai might result in our getting the books back. I need to go. I *will* go."

Mr. Parvel sighed, stepped over to the window, and stared into the evening haze. "Everything is changing so fast. Two short years, and our lives are completely different from how they used to be. How could we have prepared for this?"

Amma looked at Taemon, as though expecting him to say something here. But what?

"You're right, Mr. Parvel. Everything is changing."

Mr. Parvel turned from the window to look at him. Taemon wasn't sure where he was going with this, but he could hardly stop now.

"Amma . . . Amma has played a role in all this change — a big role. And she herself has changed, too. She's no longer a little girl." Here Taemon felt himself blushing, all too aware that he was talking to Amma's da. "But change can be a good thing, even if it makes us uncomfortable at times. Don't you think our society is better off now that we're not divided into those who have psi and those who don't? People from the city and the colony have come together and bonded over all they have in common — which was always more than what separated them, though they didn't always see that. And Amma helped make that happen.

"What we're about to do with the peace delegation will have lasting effects on generations to come. Amma should be a part of that. Who better than a Water girl to shape the landscape of the new world?"

Mr. Parvel was quiet for a moment, and Taemon let the silence work on him for a bit.

"I just . . ." Mr. Parvel said softly. "I don't know how this is going to end."

"None of us does, sir," Taemon said. "We have to create the ending. Together."

Mr. Parvel pressed his lips together and nodded. He turned to face Amma, his expression softer now. "Are you sure you're ready for this?"

She smiled and hugged her da. "A Water girl is always ready."

A few moments later, Amma walked Taemon to the door. "Thank you," she said. "You were wonderful, Mr. Knife. Mr. Cut-to-the-Quick."

Taemon scoffed. "I don't know what you're talking about."

She rolled her eyes at him, then opened the door and pushed him out. "Now get out of here. I have a million things to do to get ready."

•　　•　　•

The next day, Taemon went in search of Mam. Even though this trip wouldn't be nearly as arduous as his first foray into the Republik—for one thing, the weather would be much nicer, and Hannova would be providing plenty of food for the delegation—he still felt he should say good-bye before leaving. He headed over to Challis's house, where Mam had lived since he'd rescued her from the asylum. Da lived there, too, when he was in the colony, but he spent a lot of time in the woods with the men of Free Will, the group of rebels he'd led since The Fall. Hannova had invited them to live in the colony, but they clung to their independence and neutrality.

Nearing Challis's house, he could hear Mam's voice. The two sisters were sitting on the porch, talking. Mam was telling Challis a story, and she sounded happier than she had in a long time. Taemon lingered near the bushes on the side of the porch. They hadn't seen him yet, and he wanted to listen to Mam's story before he interrupted.

"Even back then, he was different, not like the other boys," Mam said.

Was she talking about him? Or Yens?

"I'm surprised you didn't fall for Darling Houser," Challis said. "He was quite the catch back in those days."

"Fierre? My stars, no. Fierre had such an ego. Wiljamen was much more fascinating."

Da? She was talking about Da?

"Even as a young man, his thoughts were deeper and more . . . earnest. He studied all the time. He was going to be a priest, you know. He and Naseph talked about it all the time. They were going to stick together."

Challis huffed. "Good thing they parted ways."

Had he heard that right? Da had been friends with Naseph as a boy? How was it he'd never heard that?

He must have made some sort of sound, because Mam stood up and saw him. "Taemon?"

"Just thought I'd stop by and spend a little time with you before I have to leave," Taemon said.

"Come and sit," Challis said. "I'll get you something cold to drink."

Challis went inside, and Taemon dragged another chair beside Mam. She picked up the cloth on her lap and started sewing.

"How are you feeling?" he asked.

"Better every day," Mam said. "Staying here with Challis has been just what I needed. She keeps me busy." Mam waved at the basket beside her.

Taemon lifted it into his lap and started looking through it. Shirts, dresses, hats, blankets. Mam had always been good with sewing. And cooking. That's what women did in the city—though not by hand, of course. But here in the colony, they did all sorts of jobs. It made Taemon wonder.

"Mam, if you could have any job you wanted, what would it be?"

"Oh, heavens. Such a question."

"No, really, Mam. What would you like to do?"

"I've always liked working with animals," she said.

"Maybe you should. I could talk to Bynon, out at the farm."

Mam laughed. "No, Tae. This is the perfect place for me. Challis lets me talk when I need to and hush when I need to. We're catching up on all the time we missed. And I keep my hands busy. I never would have guessed how good it feels to keep your hands busy." She knotted her thread and switched to a different color.

Challis came back and handed Taemon a cup. He took a small sip of the citrusy drink. Her odd-tasting drinks were usually steeped with herbs, and he was always a little leery of them. This one was surprisingly tasty.

"So the delegation leaves tomorrow," Challis said. "How are you feeling about going back over the mountain?"

"Okay, I guess. I just hope we can make some progress."

Challis picked up her knitting and began working on her latest scarf. "I think it's a good idea. I'm not sure it will work, but I think it's a good idea."

Taemon took another sip. He wasn't sure what to make of Challis's comment. She used to have precognition, a form of psi that gave her glimpses into the future. Her psi was gone now, but Taemon still wondered if she knew more than she let on.

Just then, Amma came running up to Challis's porch. She was nearly breathless, and she had a shoulder bag with something heavy in it. "Taemon, I need to talk to you. Can you spare a minute?"

Taemon set his drink down and gave his mother an apologetic look. "I'll be back in a bit."

"Remember the book that Vangie gave me?" Amma asked when they'd gone a little ways off. "It's all about psi, all the different forms. How they work, how they connect. Mostly I think you already know that stuff— probably better than anyone else. But after that . . . Skies, Taemon, there's some really wild stuff in that book. I don't know if it's true or if he was just some klonk-headed nutcake."

Amma was talking much faster than she usually did. And she was not the type to fluster easily.

"What kind of wild stuff?"

"He tells Nathan's story in a way I've never heard it before. If what he says is true . . ." She shook her head, unable even to complete the thought. "Let's just say it made me wonder what the Republikites' history books say about Nathan."

"From what Gevri said, they think of Nathan as a villain," Taemon said. "Someone who stole a portion of their land and weakened the soil, causing a hundred-year famine."

"And yet we revere him as a prophet, with no mention of famines or land theft. It makes me wonder if the truth is somewhere in between. This book certainly implies as much. Anyway, I think you should read the last three chapters," she said, handing him the shoulder bag. "Tonight. Before the delegation leaves."

"Okay," Taemon said doubtfully.

Amma took hold of his arm. "I know it sounds klonky, but the information in this book might just change the way people see the past. And what if that . . . what if that's powerful enough to bring peace between our two countries? Just think of it—General Sarin could change his mind, we could avoid the war, and we might even be able to get all the books back!"

Taemon frowned. "I don't know. It's not easy to change the way people see the past."

"I know, I know," Amma said. "But can it really be a coincidence that Vangie brought me this book just before we leave with the delegation? Maybe this is some sort of . . . some sort of gift."

Taemon looked at the shoulder bag, then at Amma. What if she was right? What if this was what the Heart of the Earth meant when she'd said Taemon would yet act on behalf of Deliverance?

Amma looked back at Challis's porch, and Taemon followed her gaze. Mam and Challis were watching. "I'd better get back," Taemon said.

"Read it tonight," Amma said. "We can talk about it tomorrow."

Later that night, Taemon sat in his bed with a flashlight and read the words of Kertrand Lasky:

I first met Nathan at the university, where we studied philosophy together. Even then, controversy swirled around him. He maintained that with tremendous effort and dedication, individuals could achieve a level of spiritual connection to the Heart of the Earth. This connection, claimed he, would manifest itself as extrasensory abilities. People scoffed at his lofty ideas. They scoffed, that is, until he began to showcase his psionic powers.

Even then, many believed Nathan's displays of his powers were nothing more than mere trickery. But others, myself included, were fascinated by his theories and became his followers. To us, Nathan preached principles of harmony with the earth and all people. He discovered that though he could not teach us adults how to manifest our latent psionic abilities, he could teach our young children. Words cannot express how remarkable it was to see the youngest and weakest among us communing with the Heart of the Earth in this way. Soon, we followers of Nathan had formed our own church.

We followers and admirers, however, were few. The vast majority of the population was fearful of Nathan and spoke of persecuting him—shutting down his church, banishing us all from the Republik, or worse, putting Nathan to death. Much of the church's energies were spent on reaching out to the community and working to calm fears about Nathan and his teachings.

Unlike the general population, the military saw great potential in Nathan's powers and often tried to recruit him for military projects. But Nathan refused. It went against everything he believed to use his powers to help one government make war against another. The army, however, was persistent. The Nau were spreading from continent to continent at an alarming rate, and the generals were convinced that the Republik would soon become a target.

In spite of Nathan's firm stand against the military, he believed in the Republik's right to remain independent from the Nau. He struggled with this conflict and searched for a way to assist the Republik that did not involve using psi as a weapon, which was against his principles.

After many days of solitude and contemplation, a vision came to Nathan. He saw the future of the Republik, that it would indeed fall to the Nau within five years. Nathan pleaded with the Heart of the Earth to show him a way to change the fate of the Republik. According to Nathan, the Heart of the Earth told him that there was one path that did not lead to complete Nau domination. This path, however, required drastic action and terrible sacrifice. Nathan vowed that if the Heart of the Earth would show him the path, he would do whatever was required to spare the Republik.

The path was this: the Republik must be transformed into a weak, destitute nation that would not be seen as a threat or a prize to be won. In order to do this, the Republik must endure a terrible drought that would last for generations.

Nathan debated this choice for many months, often disappearing for days and weeks at a time to further commune with the Heart of the Earth, hoping, I think, to be told of another path, one that would not cause so much suffering for his people. But as time went on and as the Nau forces grew stronger, Nathan came to believe that the Republik's only hope was for him to do as the Heart of the Earth suggested.

While he never communicated as much to me directly, I believe Nathan knew that his actions would create an unbreachable rift between his followers and the people of the Republik. Whether it was the Heart of the Earth who instructed him to raise Mount Deliverance or whether this was Nathan's idea alone, we shall never know. But our few attempts to maintain contact with our brethren back in the Republik have made it clear that they see us not as saviors but as traitors. And so we live as exiles, striving to create

a new, peaceful community here on the other side of Mount
Deliverance, until such time as old wounds have healed and
forgiveness is possible.

As Taemon read, the truth of this account came power-
fully to his mind. He understood the terrible choices
that Nathan had had to make. This explained so much
of Deliverance's past and of the centuries-old conflict
between Deliverance and the Republik. And yet the path
of the future remained dark.

The future is for you to choose. You must choose your
path, and all the consequences that follow. Once the choice
is made, you are not free to choose its effects.

The Heart of the Earth repeated those words once more
before he felt her presence withdraw.

It is for you to choose.

9 GEVRI

Gevri longed for night. He yearned for the soothing gray-
ness of evening. For the calm that came with sundown.
For a chance to let all his cares fade into blackness and
rest. He tried to imagine darkness, but even when he
closed his eyes, everything looked bright red.

They kept the lights on all the time. Bright lights.
Sometimes strobe lights.

When they stole his nights, they stole his sense of time.
His life was one continuous day, one unbroken stretch of
glaring relentless light that refused to yield to the night.

How long had his day of captivity lasted? How many days had passed in the outside world? There was no way to know. He had not been outside once since he'd been captured by the Nau.

He couldn't endure much longer.

The sleeplessness and the endless harassment made it impossible to focus his mind enough to exercise dominion, but that was irrelevant. With or without dominion, he needed to escape. Or die trying. Either option was fine by Gevri.

Gevri tried to shift his weight and grimaced with the effort. At the moment, he was chained to the wall, his arms pulled over his head. He could just barely touch the ground with his toes. If he lowered himself too far, his shoulders burned with pain. If he stood on tiptoe too long, his calves cramped with pain. The only way it was bearable was to shift the pain from one part of his body to let the other rest, and then shift again.

No sleep. Only pain.

No darkness. Only light.

When the doorknob turned and clicked, Gevri knew it was time to do something. Anything. The next person who came through that door was the person he would fight. He would give every last tick of strength in this fight. If he lived, he would be free. If not, he would die. And that was a kind of freedom, wasn't it?

The door opened, and U. Felmark Puster entered Gevri's room.

Good, Gevri thought. *Of all my tormentors, you are the one I would choose to fight.*

The investigator brought with him a folding table and took his time setting it up. He poured a cup of warm tea from a bottle. He stretched and yawned.

Is it morning? thought Gevri. *It must be morning.* Anger poured over him again, anger that he no longer had mornings. They had taken everything from him.

He allowed the anger to grow inside him. It would help him do what needed to be done.

"Hello, Gevri," Puster said. "How are you today?"

Gevri growled.

"I suppose that answers the question well enough." The investigator casually chose a file from his case, then sat on one of the stools and leafed through it. "Let's see what our topic is for today. Ah, yes, military movements."

"No!" Gevri yelled. His voice sounded hoarse and not like himself at all. "Today's topic is the archons. Where are they? What have you done to them? I'm not answering any more questions until I see them."

Puster crossed one leg over the other and set his papers on the table. He folded his hands in his lap. "Well, now, Gevri. We've discussed this before, remember? There are certain things you'll have to do to earn that privilege."

Gevri struggled to find a position that didn't split his spine with agony. He shifted this way and that, but nothing helped. "I . . . you . . . argh!"

The inspector clucked his tongue with disapproval. "Let me adjust your restraints just a bit. Perhaps we can discuss this better when you can stand on your feet."

This was a common tactic of Puster's. Gevri knew it well. Take the prisoner to an unbearable state of pain, then even the smallest act of mercy seems like kindness. This time, Gevri planned to use the tactic for his own purpose. He stopped struggling and sagged with what he hoped looked like utter defeat.

U. Felmark Puster stood up and fished a key out of his pocket, then walked over to Gevri. He fumbled with the key for a bit.

Gevri waited.

Puster jerked the chains.

Gevri waited.

Puster clicked the key in the lock.

Gevri struck. With all the strength he had left, and then some, he yanked on the chains at just the right moment, bringing the shackles on his wrists down. Down hard into Puster's forehead. The key clattered to the floor. The man crumpled.

Was he dead or unconscious? Gevri didn't care. He fell to his knees and scrambled for the key. One of the shackles had fallen off, and he used the key to remove the other. He tried the same key on the shackles around his feet and was surprised when it worked.

Completely free of chains now, Gevri bolted for the door. His knees gave out on him. His calves cramped. Every muscle protested, but he ignored them. He picked himself up and limped to the door. It didn't budge. He hobbled back to Puster and rummaged through his pockets, pulling out a ring with several keys on it. He hurried back to the door and began jamming keys into the slot. The fourth one worked.

He threw the door open and ran. Every step was agony,

but he ran down a long corridor to the next door. He jammed key after key into it until it opened. The cell was empty.

Gevri ran to the next door. This time he saw the number on the cell and took time to look for the corresponding key. An old man stared blankly at him. Gevri left the door open and hurried to the next door.

Why weren't they coming for him? Where were the guards? Half of his brain was telling him something was wrong, while the other half told him to shut up and go faster.

In the fourth cell, he found Berliott. She wasn't chained to the wall, but she was huddled in the corner, looking thin and pale. He must have looked worse, because she squinted and frowned at him. "Sir?"

"Come on." He waved her out of the cell, and she ran with him to the next. He found three more archons: Pik, Mirtala, and Wendomer.

"Do we have a plan?" Pik whispered.

"Yeah," Gevri said. "The plan is to get everyone out of here."

"Why aren't they coming?" Mirtala asked. "Why aren't the alarms sounding?"

"I don't know," Gevri said. "Just follow the plan."

The door to the next cell opened. Neeza was inside. She turned to the door, her mouth open wide with surprise.

That was the last thing Gevri saw before every light turned an ominous red. All the doors they had opened shut with a synchronized automatic motion, the locks of every door clicking at once.

"Oh, gods," one of the archons whispered behind him. "Now what?"

Gevri turned one way, then the other. There was no place to hide, just one long, empty corridor. No furniture, no nooks or crannies or cover of any kind. No windows, no ladders, nothing.

A line of Nau soldiers poured in from each side. There was nothing to do. Gevri pushed himself in front of the archons, who were pressed against the wall. He spread his arms and tried to cover them. Then he saw the guns.

Desperate, he tried to exercise dominion to disassemble the guns, but even with all the adrenaline rushing through him, he couldn't clear his mind enough to manage it. His brain was still overburdened with pain.

Then he knew what he had to do. If they shot him, he didn't want the archons in the line of fire. He stepped away from the archons until he reached the middle of the hallway. "It's me you want!" he yelled. "You've got me."

There was a moment when Gevri froze and made himself into a perfect target. *If you're going to be something, be the best,* his father had always said. It was gallows humor. This was the end.

As Gevri froze in place with his hands held high and his feet planted wide, the soldiers took their positions. Gevri picked one soldier with an oddly shaped weapon and stared directly at him. *I will not look away. I will not flinch.*

The soldier fired his weapon, but it wasn't a bullet. Time seemed to slow down as Gevri saw a steel rod spinning horizontally toward his legs. They had fired a leveler at him. *Blast it, they're not going to kill me.*

That was his last thought before the rod slammed into his legs just below the knees. Gevri went down in a heap and felt darkness closing over him.

Blessed, blessed darkness.

10 TAEMON

Taemon spent the evening before the trip helping Drigg. First they installed benches along the inside walls of the hauler. Then they removed some of the upper panels on the sides of the hauler and replaced them with wire mesh, for better air circulation.

He and Drigg worked late into the night. The work would have gone much faster with psi, but not once did Drigg bring it up. Taemon was grateful. Spending time with Drigg, working side by side on the hauler, was exactly what he needed to calm his nerves.

The delegation left before sunup. Everyone was supposed to meet at Drigg's place, which was where the hauler was parked. Amma and Mr. Parvel were the first to arrive.

"Where are your brothers?" Taemon asked. "Aren't they coming, too?"

Amma nodded. "They left yesterday, on horseback. They're checking the trail to make sure there aren't any surprises. We'll meet up with them at the end of the day."

Mr. Parvel stepped to the back of the hauler and looked inside. "Interesting work you've done there, Drigg. Is it safe?"

"Of course it's safe," Drigg said. "What do you take me for?"

While Drigg and Mr. Parvel discussed the seating arrangement, Amma pulled Taemon aside.

"Did you read the book?" she asked.

"Cha, I read it." Taemon shook his head slowly. "You were right: the truth seems to lie somewhere between our version of history and the Republik's. But do you really think the general would believe us if we told him what we know? Or that it would be enough to end a centuries-long feud?"

"I don't know," Amma whispered. "But we have to try.

If there's even the slightest chance it would help, we have to try."

A hand clasped his shoulder and squeezed. Taemon knew it was Da even before he turned to look.

"Ready for the big trip, are we?" Da said. "I'm pleased with you, son. You're becoming a real leader."

The praise caught him off guard, and he had to blink and look away. When Taemon was growing up, Da had always placed a big emphasis on humility, and praise still made him squirm a bit.

He longed to talk to Da about the new information about Nathan. Had he ever heard that part of the story? Was it true? But Mam and Challis had come to see them off, and the other delegates were arriving as well. There was no time for a private conversation.

Stepping close to him, Mam smoothed his shirt and straightened his collar—fussing seemed to come as naturally to her without psi as it had with psi. "Be careful." She gave him a thin smile, her nervousness showing in the small, stiff movements of her fingers.

Challis patted his back. "You're going to do great things. It may not seem like it at first, but this trip will be a success."

Taemon smiled and nodded. Even Challis's words of encouragement sounded like a prophecy. Some things never changed—and for that, he was grateful.

"Everybody in," Drigg called out. "Take a seat."

Amma and Taemon made their way toward the hauler.

"Yens isn't here yet," Da said.

Amma leaned toward Taemon. "Maybe we can leave without him."

They couldn't possibly be so lucky, could they? Taemon was just about to climb into the hauler when a flash of color caught his eye. He turned to see Yens riding toward them on a magnificent dappled gray horse.

When had Yens learned to ride a horse? And so competently, too? He looked at ease on the horse, with perfect posture and his usual graceful air.

With a shock, Taemon noticed that Yens had shaved his head. In Deliverance, the look was bizarre, but in the Republikite army, it was a sign of power; Gevri had shaved his head after he'd made his first kills. In addition, Yens wore a burgundy sleeveless tunic and matching pants, the collar and shoulders trimmed with orange. It was exactly the kind of clothing Taemon had seen in the Republik. Not on the soldiers, of course, who wore uniforms, but on civilians. Yens's tunic was a bit more elegant, but Taemon was certain his brother would make a strong impression with the Republikites. He looked older and wise and prestigious. He looked like a leader.

Taemon couldn't stop himself from looking down at his own dark woolen pants, his best pair, and his cleanest shirt made from blue linen. In all the preparations, the delegation had never discussed what to wear.

Yens brought his horse to a stop and dismounted with a flourish. "Good morning, everyone!"

There was a slight pause as the group took in his appearance. Yens had a pleased look on his face as he removed his bag from the saddle. A young boy, about eight years old, ran up—where had he come from?—and took the reins. Yens gave him a coin, and the boy led the horse away.

"Shall we be off?" Yens said. And everyone started moving again.

Taemon climbed into the hauler and took a seat in the corner, next to a box of food and camping supplies. Amma followed. She let out a disapproving sigh. "How does he do that?"

"He's always been that way."

The hauler quickly filled with the members of the delegation: Hannova sat next to Amma. On the other side of the hauler sat Solovar, Da, and Yens. Mr. Parvel rode next to Drigg in the front. Taemon felt the engine come to life, and the truck began to move.

Everyone in the back of the hauler seemed nervous, and Taemon knew they were thinking about the upcoming negotiations. Hannova had said that peaceful coexistence was the main issue that had to be discussed, and everyone agreed, for the most part. Amma had pushed for bringing up the books, but Hannova felt that this was at the bottom of the list. "We can bring up the stolen library only if the negotiations are going well," she'd said.

Yens, on the other hand, had wanted to emphasize commerce and trade between the two countries. He felt that the only assets Deliverance had to offer had to do with trade and natural resources. Da had objected to the idea of the Republikites cutting down the trees in Deliverance, and the two of them had argued for ages. No one wanted to get into that argument again.

The trip was much quicker and easier than when Amma and Taemon had done it last winter, especially now that they knew where the tunnel was. They ate sandwiches for lunch and took only a very short bathroom break. Soon enough they were back on the road for another long stretch, chatting about anything but the coming negotiations.

Just when they had told every riddle and played every campy guessing game, Drigg stopped the hauler. When they climbed out, Taemon saw Amma's brothers on their horses, waiting for them. He'd met them once or twice before but had never talked to them very much. They were adults now and didn't live at home anymore. One of them was married.

"Abson! Rhody!" Amma called.

"Hoy there, Pidge," Abson answered. "How was the ride? Butt a little sore?"

"Never mind about my butt," Amma said. "How are things here? Have you seen anything?"

"Everything looks fine," Rhody said. "So far, no signs that the Republikites have gone past the tunnel."

Taemon went back to help unload the camping equipment. This was as far as the hauler could take them. They would have to spend the night here, then walk the rest of the way tomorrow.

When the camping gear was unloaded, Da and Solovar

started preparing the food. Taemon and Amma had been given the job of assembling one of the two tents.

"'Pidge'?" Taemon said. "I've never heard anyone call you that before."

Amma's cheeks reddened a bit. It looked good on her. "It started off as Amma Pajama. Then somehow it ended up just Pidge."

Taemon smiled. "I get it. Pidge-Amma."

Amma reached into the bag for another stake. "Cha, something like that. But don't get any ideas. If you start calling me that, I'll think of something worse to call you." She jabbed his shoulder with the blunt end of the stake.

"I wouldn't dare," Taemon said.

The evening, night, and morning passed uneventfully. Everyone was on edge, and there was very little talking or joking. They packed up and left everything in a neat pile for Drigg to pick up the next day. Then they set off toward the tunnel.

When the sun was high above them, the trees were sparse and boulders were close together. They had to take a meandering path around the bigger ones. Mr. Parvel was leading the way, and he seemed to know where he was going, because this part looked very familiar to Taemon, even though the last time he was here, everything had been covered with snow.

"Not too much farther," Amma said. "The entrance to the tunnel is just up ahead."

Taemon did a slow spin and took in his surroundings. She was right. They should be very near the tunnel. Another half mile at the most. As he turned to face forward again, his ears began to ring. A throbbing beat started up in his head, his heartbeat pounding at his temples. In a few more steps, he felt so disoriented that he had to stop and double over.

"Stop!" Amma called to the group. Her hand was on his back.

"What's wrong, son?" Da asked.

Taemon tried to clear his head enough to stand up straight. He'd experienced this before, the last time he was in the Republik. "They're blocking my psi. They have devices that can do that by emitting sounds. There must be some of those devices hidden somewhere nearby."

Yens scoffed. "I don't hear anything."

"It's not something you can hear," Taemon said. "I'm not exactly sure how it works."

"Right," said Yens. "Sounds that you can't hear. That makes a lot of sense."

Da glared at Yens, then turned back to Taemon. "So you can't use psi at all?"

Taemon shook his head, which was a mistake. The throbbing got worse. He took a couple of short breaths and tried to maintain his composure.

"This is not acceptable," Mr. Parvel said. "We should consider turning back. Without psi as a last resort, I'm not feeling good about this at all."

"No," said Taemon. "We have to go through with this. It might be our only chance for peace."

Mr. Parvel scowled. "I'm guessing that this psi-blocking device will not prevent the Republikites from using psi, am I right?"

As much as he hated to admit it, Mr. Parvel was right. "Yes, they put something in their ears so that the device doesn't bother them."

"Which means we are no longer on equal footing. They have a huge advantage over us." He turned to Hannova with a stern look. "What would be the first step in an attack? To eliminate the leaders. They have created the perfect situation to do exactly that. I strongly recommend we turn back."

"We have to take this chance," Taemon said. "We might not get another one."

Hannova had a grim look on her face, but her voice was strong and calm. "We're going to step back out of the range of the devices while we make this decision." She led the group back along the trail. "Are we out of range?" she asked Taemon.

He nodded.

"I want to hear from each one of you," Hannova said. "Do we continue? Or do we turn back? Yens, you first."

Yens seemed pleased to be the first one consulted, but Hannova always called on the most junior member of the council first.

"I feel we must consider the possible outcomes if—"

Hannova cut him off. "No time for discussion. Go forward or turn back?"

Yens cleared his throat. "Go forward."

"Amma?"

"Go forward," Amma said without hesitation.

"Wiljamen?"

"Turn back." Da gave Taemon an apologetic look. But Taemon knew Da was only saying what he thought was best.

"Solovar?"

"Turn back."

Hannova took a deep breath. "We're going to have to turn back. We just can't risk—"

Taemon couldn't bear to hear any more. "No, please. Somebody has to take the first step of trust. I agree that we're vulnerable in this situation. There's no question that we're in the weaker position. But someone has to take the first step of trust."

He paused and was surprised that everyone seemed to be listening. So he went on. "If we turn back now, we strengthen the suspicion and distrust between our two countries. Why wouldn't we agree to meet if I didn't have use of my psi? If we turn back now, we're asking for war. And let's face it: if the war comes, we'll be annihilated."

"We beat them before," Yens said. "We can put up a good fight."

"That was one small unit of archons," Amma said.

"They have thousands of soldiers. They have guns and cannons and war machines that you've never imagined."

Taemon let Amma's words sink in before he continued. "The only chance we have to survive is to make peace, and the only chance we have to make peace is to trust. I say we go forward."

"I change my vote," Da said.

Hannova nodded. "As do I. We go forward. Cautiously!"

Mr. Parvel's frown deepened with worry, but he didn't argue. Solovar was nodding, too.

"Wish we had some of those stopper things for your ears," Mr. Parvel said.

Taemon was wishing the same thing, but he couldn't think of any way to counteract the psi-blocking device. He was just going to have to accept the fact that he couldn't use psi during the negotiations. Hadn't he just given a lofty speech about trust?

As they moved forward, the earsplitting buzzing in his head started up again, louder than before. The Republikites must have spotted the delegation from Deliverance and turned up the volume. Taemon did not want to show how much those devices were affecting him. He had to seem strong and capable. To make sure he didn't stumble as the group trudged on, he looked down, focused on the ground just ahead of his feet, and took each step carefully.

Trying to appear strong and capable led to Taemon bumping into Da, who had stopped ahead of him. Da steadied him with one arm.

"Sorry," Taemon said.

"It's okay, son," Da whispered.

Taemon looked up. They had reached the entrance to the tunnel.

Just inside the tunnel, a table had been set up, complete with a white tablecloth that ruffled gently in the draft that flowed through the tunnel. Seated at the table were eight Republikites, most of them in soldiers' uniforms.

Standing at the head of the table was General Sarin.

11 GEVRI

Gevri woke up and knew a deeper level of agony. His legs
were broken. Both of them. He knew that before he even
opened his eyes. Nothing else could hurt so badly.

Where was he? Did he even want to know? He slowly
opened his eyes and looked around.

He was in a small cell with black walls. He was lying
in the corner, his back up against a wall and his legs
stretched out on a concrete floor.

His legs. He looked down at the swollen, bruised skin.
They didn't look much like legs, other than the feet that

were at the ends of them. They were broken all right, and no one had bothered to set the bones. So this is what they had in store for him? To let him sit here and die slowly? Where were the other archons? What had happened to them?

The light was dim for a change. They weren't torturing him with strobe lights or floodlights. But then again, they didn't need to. The pain in his legs was torture enough, definitely enough to keep him from exercising dominion.

Another thought came to Gevri as he stared at the black walls. This was not an interrogation room. There was no room for U. Felmark Puster to come breezing in with his folding table and his tea. This was a cell for one person, and only one person. This was solitary confinement.

Gevri had no strength to move his body, but he turned his head and pressed his brow against the concrete wall. *They should have killed me.*

He let the sobs come, let them shake his shoulders and squeeze his ribs. *They should have killed me.*

Maybe he slept. Maybe he passed out again. Maybe he came to now and then. It was all one big blur of pain. His fevered mind was desperate to escape reality and began retelling itself old memories. Memories of his mother.

The stories that came to him were from his early years, before he had gone to live in the archon training center. He'd been three when he started living there permanently, so he knew the memories with his mother in them were very early.

She read him stories. All the good old Republikite stories about quests and heroes. Legends that no one believed anymore, about the True Son, about dragons and woodland folk. The story of Saint Stephan and the wolf-bear was his favorite, because Saint Stephan didn't hurt the wolf-bear; he just tricked him.

And tricks were what his father was teaching him. How to make things float. How to make toy cars and tanks move along their tracks without touching them. How to build castles with blocks from halfway across the room. He loved the toys and games his father brought home for him, but he loved his mother's stories more.

She read him one each night. Maybe more than one if he begged, or if he couldn't sleep, or if nightmares came. He could still remember the nightmares. Darkness gathering into the form of a person. Its eyes hollow, its mouth gaping open. Gevri would try to scream but could make no sound. He would wake up with a choking sensation, gasping and coughing.

And Mother would be there, turning on the light, saying a prayer with him, reading him another story.

He was trapped in a nightmare now, the same despair and horror gripping his chest and choking him. He struggled for air. He tried to picture his mother with him. What would she do if she were here?

She would say a prayer.

Gods, Gevri thought, *I haven't prayed since I was small.* He didn't even know if he still believed in all-knowing, all-powerful beings. He wasn't even sure he believed in the Heart of the Earth, which was about as old-fashioned as one could get. But what did he have to lose?

Whatever you are, if you are, I need help. I can't do this. I'm broken. I'm beat. If it's time for me to die, let me die. But help my archons. They're just kids. They don't deserve this. Help them. Help them. Please help them.

The death grip on his chest released, and Gevri drew in a breath.

Maybe he slept. Maybe he passed out again. Maybe he came to now and then. It was all one big blur of pain.

NAU MILITARY INTEL ADMIN LOGBOOK

> Activity Report filed by Military Investigator
U. Felmark Puster [ID# 229-8831-305]. Findings: All
observations of Republikite prisoners have been compiled
in the attached document. Data patterns indicate that
psychic blocking methods would be cost prohibitive and
impractical for wide application. <

> Recommendation: Look into adapting current technology
for use against enemies with psychic abilities. <

> Recommendation approved by the Board of Inquiry.
Copies of all relevant documents forwarded to Technology
Support. <

12 TAEMON

Hannova was the first to step forward and greet the general. She introduced herself and each member of the delegation. The general's reaction was completely neutral. No smile, no frown, no emotion at all. He kept his hands clasped behind his back and acknowledged each person from Deliverance with the smallest of nods.

There were empty chairs at the sides of the table, and one of the soldiers motioned for the delegates to take a seat. The general took his seat at the head of the table, and Hannova sat in the chair at the other end, facing him.

"There has been a misunderstanding," were the general's first words.

Taemon cringed. *Wonderful. We're getting off to a terrific start.*

General Sarin stared right at Hannova. "That seat is meant for Taemon Houser."

"Yes, there *has* been a misunderstanding," Hannova said calmly. "Taemon Houser is a member of the delegation, but I am the spokesperson."

"Taemon Houser is the only person in this group with any real power. I will speak to him. The rest of you may listen." The general spoke in a matter-of-fact tone that was as hard and cold as stone.

Taemon looked to Hannova to see what she wanted him to do. She was locked in a staring contest with the general.

Yens stood up. "Actually, I think it's me you want to talk to. Taemon pretended to be me when you saw him last. I'm the True Son, the spiritual leader of Deliverance."

The general didn't even glance at Yens. "I know who

you are. And I will discuss these matters with Taemon Houser. The others are permitted to observe."

Taemon wanted to groan. This was going even worse than he imagined.

Hannova stood and walked slowly to where Taemon was seated. She nodded to him, which seemed to be her way of giving him permission to take the lead. Reluctantly, he moved into the seat across from the general.

"We have come to discuss peace," Taemon said. He didn't know if he was supposed to speak first, but it seemed like a good idea. "We'd like to find a way for our two countries to live peacefully side by side."

General Sarin did not respond right away. This man had a gift for unnerving people in the strongest possible way.

"Our country has not known peace for many years," the general finally said. "You are aware, of course, of the war that wages between the Nau and the Republik."

"Yes," Taemon said. "I am aware. We wish to remain neutral."

The general continued. "There is no neutral. The Nau will come to Deliverance. Maybe next month, maybe next year. But they will most certainly come. Deliverance is small. It is powerless. It is weaponless. It will fall. The question is this: Will Deliverance fall to the Republik or to the Nau? My job is to ensure that Deliverance is occupied by the Republik, not by the Nau. I'm sure you understand."

Taemon did not know what to say to that.

The general smiled, and that was even more unnerving than his brusque manner. "Now you see that the peace we will be discussing is the peaceful occupation of Deliverance by the Republik."

Taemon finally found his voice. "No, General Sarin. We are not willing to give in so easily. We are a peaceful people. This war is not ours."

"I see," the general said. "You believe it is possible to be left alone. That the Nau will not seek to occupy you."

"Yes," Taemon answered.

"I can assure you that that is not the case. Deliverance is geographically significant; whoever rules your city also controls the ports to either side. If the Nau gain control of Deliverance, the Republik is all but lost. But if the Republik were to occupy your city, we would be positioned to launch defensive strikes against our enemy.

"In short, war is coming to Deliverance whether you

want it to or not. If you allow the army of the Republik to occupy Deliverance, we will defend your land for you. Gods know you cannot defend it on your own."

Skies, this was all so complicated! Taemon was tempted to look to Hannova for help, but that would show weakness. He needed to appear strong. Deep in his gut, he knew it was a mistake to let the Republik into Deliverance. Once they were there, they would never leave. Deliverance would be swallowed up by the Republik. If the Nau came, they would find a way to deal with that.

"Thank you for your offer, but we must decline," Taemon said. "We will put our trust in the Heart of the Earth and fend for ourselves."

The general's look turned stone cold again. "Doesn't that sound just like a Nathanite?"

Taemon sat up straighter. "You mean to insult me, General, but I take the comparison as the highest compliment. Nathan was forced to make an impossible decision for the good of the people—for the good of the Republik—and though your history books have tarnished his reputation, I am proud to be the descendant of such a man, and prouder still to be compared to him."

The general scoffed. "And your history books have

made an idol out of a traitor! Nathan could have fought with the Republik and wiped out the Nau in its infancy. Instead, he turned his back on us, stole our land, and hid his people behind this very mountain. For centuries, we have paid the price of his so-called neutrality. If you continue to follow Nathan's path—the coward's path—the Republik will have no choice but to take Deliverance by force."

"There is much that both our history books have left out," Taemon acknowledged, returning the general's icy stare. "But know this: Nathan's path was *not* the coward's path. Only a narrow-minded fool would see it that way. And so we choose to follow Nathan's path and do what is best for our people."

The general laughed, startling the delegates from Deliverance. "You are asking me to leave you in peace! As if you can get what you want by saying 'please.' You have nothing to bring to the bargain, not one thing. And you are asking me to risk *my* people by leaving yours alone."

"What do you want?" asked Taemon. "Other than our land?"

The general grew serious. He placed his hands on the table and leaned forward. "There is something you can do. Something to show me that you are powerful enough to withstand the Nau."

"What is it?" Taemon was certain he wasn't going to like anything that General Sarin asked for.

The general leaned back in his chair. "You are acquainted with my son, Gevri, are you not?"

Taemon felt his stomach clench into knots. Where was this going? "Yes, I am."

"Gevri has been taken prisoner by the Nau. He is being held in a stronghold near Lake Simawah. If you will go there and free him, I will honor your request to leave Deliverance alone."

Gevri? In a Nau prison? "You have plenty of other archons. Why do you need me?"

"The group of misfit archons that you worked with at Kanjai—you remember them as well, I assume?" The general's look was steely cold, and his voice gave away no emotion.

"Of course I do," Taemon answered.

"They have been captured as well. Gevri and his unit, they are all very young. By now, I fear they have given the Nau the answers they are looking for. If the Nau under-stand how we use dominion, they will undoubtedly begin looking for a way to counteract it. I cannot afford to send any more archons to the Nau until I know what they have learned." The general nodded to one of his soldiers, who immediately laid a map on the table and shoved it toward Taemon.

"Lake Simawah is about seven hundred miles northwest of here," the general said. "I will provide a vehicle and a driver."

Taemon looked at the map, but it meant little to him. Seven hundred miles? In a vehicle driven by one of the general's men? Whether Gevri and the other archons were really imprisoned or not, Taemon could hardly ignore the fact that this would be a convenient way of getting him out of the picture so the general could invade Deliverance without any resistance. What was it that the general had said when the delegation first arrived? That Taemon was the only one with any power? Taemon was the only person standing in the general's way of taking over Deliverance.

Taemon folded the map and slipped it into his pocket. "I'm sorry, General. I can't leave right now. As you yourself explained, Deliverance is vulnerable at the moment. We could be attacked at any time. I cannot abandon my people."

The general rose to his feet. "Then we have nothing more to discuss. I will honor the protocol of allowing the delegation to return to your land in peace. In due time, we shall meet again on the battlefield."

"Understood," Taemon said.

"Wait just a minute," Yens said. "I'll go to Lake Simawah. I'll rescue your son. I'm sure we can come to an agreement somehow."

Hannova took Yens's arm and tried to lead him away, but he yanked his arm out of her grasp. "We can't just let him —"

"The discussion is over," the general boomed. "If you break the protocol of leaving peacefully, you invite us to break it as well."

In a heartbeat, the soldiers unholstered their weapons and stood with the guns held against their chests. It was a show of force, an open display of weapons with no direct threat. Yet.

"We are leaving peacefully," Mr. Parvel said to the group from Deliverance. "Now!"

On the way back to Deliverance, the mood in the hauler was grim.

"Now we have to go back and prepare for war," Hannova said. "We've done everything we could."

"Have we?" Yens turned to Taemon. "I don't understand why you don't just use psi to crush those war machines you keep talking about. Or for that matter, you can just kill that insufferable Sarin. If I were you, I would just reach into his heart and . . . *ungh!*" Yens made a squeezing motion with his fist to illustrate.

The others in the hauler stared at Taemon with wide eyes.

"You can do that?" Hannova asked.

Taemon looked at his feet.

"Of course he can," Yens said. "All I know is, if I had telekinesis, and remote viewing, and clairvoyance, I would use every one of them together and kill all the soldiers before they even set foot in Deliverance."

"I could," Taemon said, not looking up. "But I won't. Psi is not meant to do harm to others. Nathan knew this. It's why he was exiled."

"Exiled!" Yens said. "Nathan *chose* to leave Republik. They were ignorant fools who didn't realize how powerful he was. He left to start his own society of psi wielders. And if you hadn't gotten rid of psi for everyone but yourself, we'd be the invincible society Nathan had envisioned and there'd be no talk of wars or invasions!"

Taemon was about to launch into an explanation of what he'd recently learned about Nathan, but he felt Da pat him on the back. "You are right about Nathan, son. His way was the way of peace. If we die, we die without anyone else's death on our conscience."

Yens scoffed. "If anyone in Deliverance dies because you didn't defend them, won't that be on your conscience?"

As the argument became more heated, Taemon cradled his head in his hands, rocking gently. What should he do? What was his duty?

You will yet act on behalf of the people of Deliverance.

I did act! Taemon protested. *But the negotiations failed miserably. General Sarin is determined to invade Deliverance. And if he doesn't, the Nau surely will.*

You will yet act.

What action was left? What could he do? Deliverance was caught between two fearsome forces that were intent on annihilating each other. So long as their city remained geographically valuable, the people would never be safe.

Suddenly an idea came to Taemon. It was crazy. It was desperate. But . . .

Will it work? he asked. *Is this what you had in mind?*

The Heart of the Earth was silent for so long that Taemon had nearly given up on hearing back. Then: **The future is for you to choose. You must choose your path, and all the consequences that follow. Once the choice is made, you are not free to choose its effects.**

Hardly the ringing endorsement that he'd hoped for. But Taemon knew the Heart of the Earth spoke the truth. All he could do was try his best; the rest was outside of his control.

Taemon interrupted the argument that was still going strong. "We must leave Deliverance. As soon as we get back, we will tell the people to pack everything up. We'll move everyone out of the way of the fighting."

That quieted them.

"Leave everything?" Hannova said.

"We can't just hand it over to the Republik!" Yens said.

"Or the Nau," added Solovar.

But Da was nodding. "It's not an easy solution, but it might work. It's better than trying to fight when you're the only one without a weapon."

"The people won't like it," said Solovar.

Amma huffed. "They'll like it better than war."

"I don't know," Hannova mumbled. "I'm not sure we have time. . . ."

"I'm not leaving," Yens said. "I'm going to stay and fight for my country."

Solovar nodded. "We've worked so hard to rebuild it."

"We can rebuild it somewhere else," Da said. "After all, Nathan led his people out of their land and into Deliverance." He looked hopefully at Taemon. "Do you have a place in mind, somewhere we will be safe?"

All eyes looked at him. Slowly Taemon shook his head. "I don't yet know where we should go. All I know is that leaving is our only option."

Immediately the group started grumbling again — Yens the loudest of them all.

Drigg cut in. "As soon as we get home, I'm going to start packing," he said. "Just in case."

The bickering continued, but Taemon tuned out the discussion. He knew he should be thinking about the next steps of this crazy plan of his, but he couldn't stop thinking about what the general said about Gevri and the other archons being held prisoner by the Nau. Was that a lie meant to lure Taemon away from Deliverance? Or could it be true?

He felt in his pocket for the map that showed how to get to Lake Simawah.

Could it be true?

It was dark when they finally arrived in Deliverance. Mr. Parvel told Amma she could go home while he stayed to help unload the truck.

"No, thanks," she said. "I'll stay and help."

She and Taemon carried the tents into Drigg's workshop.

"I'm sorry we didn't get to talk about the books at all." He dropped the tent on the floor and stirred up a bit of sawdust.

Amma shrugged. "It wasn't the right time, I know. But I actually think it worked out for the best."

"What do you mean?"

"I've been thinking about it, and if there's going to be a war here, the books are probably safer in the Republik. And if we have to evacuate, there's no way we could take loads of books with us."

They dropped the tents onto the workshop floor and went back to the truck.

"When this is all settled," Amma said, "I *will* find those books. And you're going to help me."

"Yes, sir," Taemon replied with a salute.

Back at the truck, Drigg handed them each a box that contained cooking utensils. They turned around and headed to the workshop. They discussed the meeting with the general, and Taemon asked the question that had been puzzling him all day.

"Do you think Gevri is really in prison?"

"I'm not sure," Amma admitted. "It could've been a ruse. But if it's not . . ." She frowned. "What I can't figure out is why the general asked you to free Gevri. Admitting he needs help doesn't seem like something he would do."

"It must be a trap," Taemon concluded, setting the cookware down with a rattle. It would be just like the general to invent some horrible lie about Gevri and the other archons being held prisoner—being interrogated or even tortured—in order to manipulate Taemon into leaving Deliverance undefended.

Suddenly he remembered the message that Jix had delivered. She had been in a cage, starved and tortured and waiting to die. Till Gevri had shown up and helped her escape.

Had the jaguar been trying to tell him that *Gevri* was locked up and needed someone to save him, just as he'd saved her? Was the general telling the truth?

He couldn't risk leaving Deliverance, leaving his people vulnerable to attack.

But what if there was another way to save Gevri and the others—and secure peace between Deliverance and the Republik?

NAU MILITARY INTEL ADMIN LOGBOOK

> Activity Report filed by Military Investigator
U. Felmark Puster [ID# 229-8831-305]. Status Update:
The Republikite prisoners have been classified as
expendable. <

> Recommendation: Elimination. <

> Prisoner elimination approved. <

13 GEVRI

Gevri's legs were getting worse. He couldn't even bear to move them. He felt hot and sweaty, and he knew what that meant: infection. Someone shoved food into his cell once a day, but Gevri didn't even bother to eat. He was dying; that was certain. Why prolong it by eating?

He drifted in and out of reality, sometimes reliving memories, sometimes redreaming nightmares, waiting for death to claim him. It was all a jumbled haze of pain, until something came to him.

Gevri could not say what it was, exactly. It did not feel like the other hallucinations he'd experienced. This time, he was fully aware of what was happening, more aware than he had been during his entire captivity.

Someone was with him. He felt a distinct presence here, in this dank misery of a cell.

Taemon.

He knew it with more certainty than if he'd actually seen him with his eyes. He knew it the same way he could feel Saunch or Neeza in his head with telepathy—though he hadn't been able to detect them since their capture. He just knew who it was, the way he knew when he tasted mustard or smelled the ocean.

It was Taemon. Not physically in the room, but his influence, his dominion, was here.

At first, nothing changed other than the feeling that he was not alone anymore. Gevri had a feeling that Taemon was watching, searching, observing and probing.

When something did happen, it was excruciating. Gevri felt the bones in his left leg shift. He couldn't stop himself from crying out. Then a burning sensation began, like a fire deep in his bones. Gevri was pretty sure what was happening. His bones were knitting themselves back together. Sure enough, once the agony had subsided, his leg looked straight again, his foot angled the way it should.

The same thing repeated in the other leg. First the stab of exquisite pain—Gevri only gasped this time—then the burning. Now both legs looked straight.

After that, Gevri watched with wonder as the swelling in his legs disappeared in a matter of seconds. Bruises, crusty wounds, lacerations—they all healed themselves and disappeared with only the faintest of scars left on his skin.

A surge of energy blazed through his legs and moved throughout his body. His dizziness and fever dissipated. He felt good. No, not good. Perfect. Not even hungry or tired.

He stood, something he never thought he would do again. He flexed his legs. He felt like he could do a set of military three-a-day workouts without breaking a sweat.

Taemon was doing this? If Taemon was this powerful, why had he not shown it before?

If the miracle of his legs was not enough, Gevri could

not believe the next thing he saw. The door to his cell swung open.

Taemon? Is it you? How? Why?

You freed Jix, Taemon answered. *Your father asked me to free you.*

After that, Gevri felt Taemon's presence withdraw.

Gevri hesitated, recalling what had happened the last time he tried to escape. Then he realized: now that he was fully healed, he could exercise dominion freely. He lifted his shoulders and strode out the door.

Immediately a line of Nau soldiers approached him head-on. He waved his hand and dismantled all their guns, then shoved the soldiers backward out the door. As he walked down the hall with confident strides, he lifted the hinges from each door he passed. Some of the cells were empty. Then he found Saunch. Then Mirtala. They were dazed and pale, but they could walk.

Another squadron of soldiers came at him from behind, but taking away their guns was all too easy. He broke down each gun, sent it into an empty cell, then replaced the locked door. He pushed the soldiers into another cell and locked them in.

The archons made their way down the length of the

hall, easily dispatching any resistance they met. The last archon he found was Cindahad. He had to carry her.

They walked out of the building and met snipers on the rooftops, three fat pigs, and even a small tank. Gevri felt invincible. Nothing could touch him. Nothing would stop him. Taking long, deliberate steps, he exercised dominion as strongly as he ever had. He raised a force field, a bubble around his archons and himself. Bullets pinged and fell in the opposite direction. He tipped the fat pigs upside down and bent their snouts. He made the tank explode.

The archons didn't say anything, didn't whimper or flinch. They just followed him.

Gevri and every one of his archons walked out of the Nau stronghold. When they were far enough away, he let them rest. Pik was the only archon besides Gevri who was strong enough to summon dominion. Using remote viewing, he found the nearest cluster of Republikite army spies. When they were ready, Gevri and the archons walked another hour and joined them.

They were given food, water, medical attention, and, best of all, a place to sleep.

Then came the questions.

"You just walked out of the Nau's Lake Simawah stronghold?"

"Impossible!"

"How did you do it?"

And Gevri gave them the only honest answer he could: "I don't know."

```
NAU MILITARY INTEL ADMIN LOGBOOK

> Activity Report filed by Military Investigator
U. Felmark Puster [ID# 229-8831-305]. Status Update:
Republikite prisoners have escaped. Casualty report
will follow. <

> Requests: Two additional security units. <

> Board of Inquiry requests copies of surveillance
recordings. Request for additional security approved. <
```

14 TAEMON

Two days had passed since Taemon had stretched his psi to its limits and reached across seven hundred miles to heal Gevri and help him escape. He'd had to use every ability he had to make it happen — remote viewing to see what was happening in the Nau stronghold near Lake Simawah, clairvoyance to see Gevri's injuries, telekinesis to heal them and to open the cell door, and even telepathy to communicate with Gevri briefly.

He'd already told Hannova's council about what he'd done, though he asked them to keep it confidential. The last thing he wanted was to spread false hope among the people of Deliverance. But he fully expected a message of some kind from the general in the next few days, saying that he would honor the agreement of peace.

Rescuing Gevri had wiped him out for an entire day. He wished he could have communicated more with Gevri at the time, but after healing both his legs and the infection in his body, then looking into the lock mechanism in his cell door and opening the lock, Taemon had been exhausted. He simply didn't have any extra energy to put into a long telepathic chat.

Now that Taemon had fully recovered, maybe it was time to have that chat.

That evening, as Taemon lay in his bed, he reached out with remote viewing to try to find Gevri. If he was in Kanjai, he might be able to locate him. Taemon closed his eyes and called on psi to stretch his awareness. Farther, farther, over the mountain, through the tunnel, into Kanjai, inside the archon facility. His psionic perception drifted from room to room, never looking too closely, never lingering too long.

And there.

There was Gevri.

In a room with books.

A library perhaps? No, it looked more like a storeroom. Gevri was searching through boxes of books. He selected a volume, took it to a corner where a pile of packing blankets were stacked, and sat down to read it. Taemon tried to zero in on the book, curious to know what Gevri was reading, but he couldn't get his awareness to travel close enough for him to read the title.

But a thought struck him. Were these books *Amma's* books? Even if he could read the titles, he didn't have a way of knowing if they were hers. And yet something told him that they were.

Gevri settled himself on the blankets and leafed through the book.

He looked up suddenly.

Taemon, is that you?

Yes. I am sorry to intrude, but I'm afraid it's important. Have you told your father what happened? That I rescued you from the Nau prison as he asked?

I'm not ready to talk about it yet.

He said if I rescued you, he wouldn't attack Deliverance. He needs to know that I helped you so he'll live up to that bargain.

I'm grateful for what you did. But I don't control my father. I think you know that.

Gevri, I know that you respect and fear your father. But I also know that a part of you doubted him at one time— doubted that his plan was the right one. Listen to that part of you, Gevri. You have the ability to defy your father, to stop this war. Think about what is best for the Republik. Then do it! Don't be afraid of the consequences.

There was a long pause, and Taemon began to wonder if Gevri was even listening anymore. Did he have a way of shutting Taemon out?

When Gevri's answer finally came, it came forcefully, the telepathic equivalent of yelling. *You know nothing! The boy that you speak of, the boy full of doubts, is no longer. I am wiser now, and stronger. And I see that what is best for the Republik is to eradicate the scourge known as the Nathanites!*

Taemon felt the connection between him and Gevri break abruptly. It was almost painful, like a door being slammed in his face. He had to take a moment to gradually withdraw his perception and return all his faculties to his immediate surroundings. It took him a few more moments to process what he'd learned.

Gevri was not going to go against his father. If Taemon couldn't resolve his conflict with Gevri, what hope did they ever have of getting through this? There was nothing else to do but evacuate all of Deliverance.

Taemon didn't sleep very well at all. After his conversation with Gevri, Taemon knew he couldn't depend upon General Sarin to show the people of Deliverance any mercy, even though Taemon had gone ahead and freed his son.

As soon as the sun was up, he hurried to Hannova's house and banged on the door in spite of the early hour.

It was her husband, Sansom, who opened the door, looking bleary-eyed.

"Sorry," Taemon said. "But I need to talk to Hannova."

"She's gone already," Sansom said. "She's visiting the fishing camp this morning, taking a look at their new setup. She won't be back until this afternoon."

Taemon frowned. "Could you tell her to come find me as soon as she gets back? It's urgent."

He hurried back to the workshop. Drigg would travel

into the city today for the weekly delivery of supplies. Taemon would tag along; with luck, he'd run into Solovar there and see what the elder man thought of his idea.

Around the midday break, Taemon made his way to the temple, which was nothing more than a large pile of stones. Still, it served as a gathering place for the people— as much out of habit as anything else, he suspected. Before The Fall, the high priest would stand on the temple balcony to address the people who gathered in the court-yard below. The balcony was long gone, but about half of the large flat stones that formed the courtyard remained intact, and Yens had taken to preaching to the people from there. Despite whatever rumors were floating about Yens's lack of psi, he still managed to draw a sizable crowd.

"The Heart of the Earth is with us," Yens was saying as Taemon approached. "Once again the people of Nathan have been delivered!"

The crowd rustled with energy.

"Recently I led the peace delegation that met with the Republikite general. At first, there was much anger and hostility. The general was intent on attacking us."

Murmurs of alarm came from the listeners.

"Then we learned that the general's son was in danger. He had been captured by their enemies. I offered to save his son in return for an agreement of peace between the Republik and Deliverance."

Frustration began to simmer inside of Taemon. Now that Yens was attending the weekly meetings, he had learned of Gevri's rescue when Taemon had reported it to the council, and Yens was using that to his own advantage. This was exactly how Yens operated: most of what he said was true, but he twisted the truth to make himself come out the hero.

"Now the general's son has been rescued, which has restored peace to Deliverance. I can assure you that there is no reason to fear the Republikite army now. The Heart of the Earth has provided a way for us to live in harmony with the Republik! We shall continue to rebuild our lands and our homes! We shall prosper, as the people of Nathan have always prospered!"

The crowd cheered and gave voice to their gratitude. Yens was their savior! Yens was the True Son! Yens would safeguard the people of Deliverance!

Taemon hadn't had a chance to tell the council that the rescue had softened neither Gevri nor his father. Taemon could not stand still and listen to his brother fill the people with a false sense of security. He skirted around the edge of the crowd and jumped atop one of the stones near Yens. "I beg you all to listen! I'm afraid that what Yens has told you isn't the truth. Deliverance is still under threat of attack."

Yens turned and threw him a look of rage. "We had a deal, Taemon," he growled, too low for the crowd to hear.

"This is not about who gets the glory," Taemon whispered to his brother. "The general could very well attack! We need to warn people!"

"So, then, what do you propose, dear brother?" Yens asked, his voice falsely sweet—and loud enough now for the crowd to hear.

"The only way we can survive this is if we leave Deliverance."

The crowd gasped and murmured in alarm.

Yens was quick to respond. "This is our homeland— land carved out for us by our founder, Nathan. Land given to Nathan and his people by the Heart of the Earth. It is our sacred duty to protect this land!"

The crowd cheered their approval.

"We have no choice!" Taemon said. "The Republikite army *will* attack—and when they do, we will have no way to protect ourselves. Our only option is to leave." He spoke directly to the crowd now. "Pack up only what you need to survive! We must move quickly!"

Confusion and fear spread among the crowd.

Yens turned to Taemon. "You *could* defeat them," he muttered, "but you choose not to. That is why you are not the True Son." He beat one fist against his chest. "I am the True Son!" he bellowed. "And I will stay! I will fight! I will die defending my country and my people, if that is what is asked of me!"

The crowd roared their agreement. With fists in the air, they began to chant, "We will stay! We will fight! We will stay! We will fight!"

Yens jumped off the temple stone, his tunic fluttering in the descent, and made his way through the crowd. They followed, repeating the chant as he marched them through the streets of the city. "We will stay! We will fight!"

And you will die, Taemon added silently.

It was late afternoon before Hannova could assemble the council for an emergency meeting. Drigg had found Solovar, and he had ridden with them back to the colony for the meeting.

"My guess is that many people are going to follow Yens and stay in Deliverance," Solovar said once the group was assembled.

"They don't understand what they'll be facing," Amma said. "These people cannot even conceive of the destruction the Republikite army will bring."

"As much as we'd like to, we can't force them to evacuate," Hannova said. "All we can do is our best. I will send runners to the fishing and lumber camps. Mr. Parvel, I need you to assemble your volunteer security force and get the word out to everyone in the colony. Tell them they can't bring very much. Only absolute necessities. We need to be able to travel as quickly as possible."

"There is one big question we haven't discussed," Da said. "Where are we going?"

"Yes," Hannova said. "Where will we go?"

All eyes turned to Taemon. He gave them the only honest answer he could: "I don't know."

The silent despair in the room was unbearable. "But I will figure it out," Taemon added. "By tomorrow morning, I will figure it out."

NAU MILITARY INTEL ADMIN LOGBOOK

> Casualty Report 381/92 filed by Military Investigator
U. Felmark Puster [ID# 229-8831-305]. Summary: 53 deceased,
28 injured. <

> Recommendation: Performance Review for Military
Investigator U. Felmark Puster [ID# 229-8831-305]. <

> Board of Inquiry requests copies of surveillance
recordings. Request for additional security approved.
Performance Review approved and scheduled for Military
Investigator U. Felmark Puster [ID# 229-8831-305]. <

15 GEVRI

With Jix beside him, Gevri had fallen asleep while reading the book. Since he'd returned to Kanjai, Jix would not
leave his side. Her presence, her strength, and her companionship were the things that helped the most as Gevri
struggled to deal with the memories of the Nau prison
that haunted him. Jix was the one who stayed with him
during the long, sleepless nights. Jix, who never asked
questions, never passed judgment.

Gevri's father shook him awake.

"I thought I might find you here." The general pulled up a crate and sat. Jix sat up and eyed the general closely, as she did everyone around Gevri.

Gevri slowly leaned forward and tried to straighten his posture as much as he could on a shifting pile of packing quilts. He rubbed his eyes and tried to focus.

"At ease," the general said.

"I wish I could get into a sleep schedule," Gevri said. "All those days of deprivation, and all I wanted to do was sleep. But now when I want to sleep, I can't. Then I fall asleep when I don't mean to."

"Another day or two and you'll be fine. Just in time to lead the attack on Deliverance." His father rested a hand on Gevri's shoulder. "I want you to know I'm very proud of you. Not very many soldiers could have stood up to that. And the way you broke out of that prison, that was remarkable. They'll be telling that story for generations to come."

"About that . . ." Gevri said. He and his father hadn't had much of a chance to talk privately since Gevri had returned to Kanjai. "I need to tell you how that happened."

"I know what happened," the general said.

"No, you don't. It was Taemon. He came in with his psi, and he—"

"Stop right there." The general held up a palm. "Taemon was nowhere near Lake Simawah. I have soldiers posted as lookouts in the mountains, and they assure me that no one has left Deliverance."

Gevri shook his head. "He wasn't in the room, but his psi was there."

The general let out a booming laugh. "That's ridiculous. No one can use psi over that much distance."

Jix let out a low warning growl.

"That's what I thought," Gevri said. "I came down here to look through these books and see if there's anything written about using psi from a distance. Look here, Father. It says that—" Gevri leafed through the book to find the page he had been reading.

The general reached over and put his hands gently over Gevri's. Then he closed the book and set it back into an open crate. "Let me tell you what happened. You were hallucinating. This is what happens with severe sleep deprivation. Your mind can't distinguish between reality and dreams. I know that Taemon has been on your mind ever since you met him last winter. Am I correct?"

"Yes, but—"

The general raised his hand. "Taemon has been on your mind. Perhaps, on a level deeper than your everyday awareness, perhaps you feel guilty about attacking Deliverance. So your mind created this story in which Taemon saved you, furthering your subconscious belief that the attack on Deliverance was wrong. I assure you, though, that Taemon had nothing to do with your rescue. You rescued yourself."

"How can you be sure?" Gevri asked, stroking Jix's head.

"Because I spoke to him. Not with dominion, or *psi*," he said that word with disgust. "I spoke to him person-to-person. I asked him to save you, and he refused."

Gevri leaned forward and rested a hand on his father's knee. "That's what he said! He said you asked him. Did you make an agreement to withdraw the attack if he rescued me?"

The general stiffened. "No agreement was reached. I made a request; he refused. We owe him nothing, Gevri. If they would allow us to occupy Deliverance peacefully, we would do so. But they refuse."

The general stood up and paced the room. "This is all very normal, Gevri. This is your brain's way of surviving a traumatic experience. But I need you to understand that this is a fictional version of what took place. Here is the truth: once your legs were broken, and you were close to death, your body and spirit rallied with one great effort to free yourself. There are documented cases of this in our research. All the power of dominion that had been suppressed during your captivity gathered itself and burst to the surface. You healed yourself, Gevri. Your brain needed a way to convince you that this was possible, so you told yourself that Taemon was doing it. But Taemon did not heal you, Gevri. He did *not*."

A quiet moment passed as Gevri tried to make sense of his father's explanation. The general stood by a window and looked out, hands clasped behind his back. Jix shifted her lean body and moved closer to Gevri's leg, then rested her chin on her paws.

He tried to remember what had happened in the Nau prison. Some of it was too horrific to think about. But he did remember hallucinating, and sometimes Taemon was part of those hallucinations. The healing, though—the healing was different. Taemon's presence had felt so real.

He wasn't sure he could accept what his father was telling him. But his father had no cause to lie to him. They were working together now. The days when they were at odds with each other—the days of Gevri's rebelliousness and pride and of his father's lies and manipulations—were over. He was not about to bring them back.

Besides, even if Taemon had healed him—and that was a big if—then it was probably another trick to make Gevri think that Taemon was his friend, to get Gevri to convince his dad to call off the war. Hadn't Taemon admitted as much? It was the move of someone who was desperate—someone who knew just how weak he and his people were.

"Let's speak no more of this," his father said. "It's time to move forward with the attack. Do you feel up to attending the planning meeting?"

The general was right. It was time to move on. Did it really matter how he had escaped? Whether Taemon had done it or Gevri had done it, that didn't change anything. Gevri stood up and stretched. "I wouldn't miss it."

• • •

The planning meeting didn't start for another hour, and Gevri planned to spend that time with his unit. They had each been through their own terrible ordeals, and spending time together was a way to recuperate and feel united again. And he knew exactly what to do.

"A run?" Saunch asked. "Are you fuzzed?"

"Come on," Gevri said. "It'll be fun."

"Are you giving us an order?" Mirtala asked.

"I was hoping I wouldn't have to. Just a quick jog through the equipment yard."

It took a little persuasion, but in the end, they all came, Jix included.

Gevri took the lead with Jix at his side. He jogged around the equipment, dodging outdated motorcycles and mini tanks, the other archons following behind him in single file. This was where all the outdated equipment was stored before being stripped for parts or scrap metal.

They played an old game called "Three Tricks." The leader had to do some kind of little maneuver, like jumping over something or running backward for a few paces, then everyone in the line had to do the same thing. Anyone who didn't successfully complete the trick had to go to the back of the line. Once the leader had completed three tricks, he or she moved to the end of the line, and a new leader took over.

When they were all worn out, Gevri led them out of the equipment yard and into a little grove of trees.

"All halt!" Gevri called, and they each found a grassy spot to rest. "Drink water! That's an order."

Gevri took a gulp of water, then poured some in a bowl for Jix to drink. He actually enjoyed the soreness in his legs. For a while, he had been convinced he would never again be able to run and wear out his muscles like this.

"Do we have to go back?" Saunch asked. "I don't want to go to that planning meeting."

"I know the meetings are boring, but they're necessary," Gevri said. "So, yes, we have to go back."

Saunch picked at the grass in front of him. "Do we really have to attack Yens?"

Gevri looked around and saw questioning looks from the others as well.

"His name is Taemon," Gevri said. "And we've talked about this before. An enemy is an enemy."

"I'm still going to call him Yens," Cindahad said.

Gevri laughed. Taemon would hate that. "Be my guest."

After an uneasy silence, Gevri sensed that the archons were still conflicted. "Look, it has nothing to do with Taemon. What do you think is going to happen when the Nau figure out that Deliverance has no more power? They're going to move in quicker than you can sneeze. Do you really want a Nau army just over that mountain? Have you heard the reports? The Nau are moving closer on the west, too. You can see exactly what they're trying to do: send one army from the west and another from Deliverance, in the east. They're going to trap us in the middle. How long do you think we can withstand that?"

All the archons were looking down. Wendomer was screwing the cap of her water bottle on and off. Mirtala was breaking a twig into little pieces. Berliott was braiding strands of grass. But Gevri knew they were listening.

"This is not about Taemon. This is about the Nau. The ones who captured us. The ones who tortured us. The ones who would have killed us. If we lose this battle, we lose the war. Are we united in our mission?" Gevri saw a few weak nods. He jumped to his feet. "Are we united?"

The archons stood with him. "Cha!"

He started jogging through the trees. "Are we united?"

"Cha!" came the chorus behind him, and a respectable roar from Jix.

He led them back to the archon training center, doing three tricks along the way. Every archon mimicked him perfectly.

16 TAEMON

"Do you want me to go with you?" Amma said.

Taemon had come to the workshop just long enough to shove a few things in his knapsack: a water bottle, a flashlight, a blanket—he didn't need much more. He was going to the mountain to ask the Heart of the Earth where the people of Deliverance should go. He just hoped she had an answer.

Taemon shook his head. "I need to do this alone. And you need to pack."

Amma frowned. "Are you sure this can't wait till morning?"

Taemon shook his head. "I can't explain it; I have this feeling that we need to leave tomorrow. But first I need to know where we're going." He flung his bag over his shoulder.

She followed him to the door. He looked at her, and a strange mix of emotions swirled in his chest. He felt as though there were a million things that he wanted to say to her, but no words came.

"All right, well . . ." Amma patted his shoulder. "Safe travels."

Taemon nodded and looked down. He had to turn away from her before he embarrassed himself with klonky words that wouldn't make sense.

Dusk had brushed the mountain with a pink-gray light. Taemon followed the trail, then cut through the dry end-of-summer grass toward his giant old ruddybark tree. Honestly Taemon was glad to have some time alone. The hours following the emergency meeting had been frustrating.

The council had gone in pairs to spread the word to all the colonists. Everyone had to be ready to evacuate by noon the next day. Everywhere they went, people had questions and arguments and complaints about having to leave so suddenly, but the council members were short on answers. No, they didn't know when the army would be here. No, they didn't have any more details. And most of all, no, they didn't know where they were going.

Many of the people flatly refused to leave. *Don't waste time asking questions!* he wanted to shout at them. *Just get ready!* The sad thing was, Taemon didn't have time to stop and try to persuade them. He barely had time to knock on all the doors in his assigned route.

Yes, a walk on the mountain was just what he needed right now.

By the time Taemon got to his tree, it was nearly dark, but he didn't bother with the flashlight. He lay there under the tree and let the night sounds wash away the fear. The frogs that trilled from the creek didn't have any worries. The insects whining around his head didn't have any troubles. He stilled his mind until there was only this tree. This sky. This moment.

When he was ready to listen, he was ready to ask.

I'm willing to do what I must to save my people. I'm ready to lead them out of Deliverance. Please tell me where we can go.

Nothing came to him.

Patient. He had to be patient. He had to be still and listen.

Still nothing came.

What could he do? Pout? Demand an answer?

No, he could only wait. He would wait all night if he had to.

He tried not to think about how long he'd been there, but it had been a long time. Maybe it was the darkness, or maybe the worries were too great to keep at bay for very long. Taemon could feel despair creeping into him.

And with despair came its companion, doubt.

Was he leading the people to safety? Or was he cowering from opposition? Was he really the True Son?

Once started, the doubts flooded his thoughts like a cloud of bats. They gathered and multiplied and swarmed until he could barely breathe.

Was the Heart of the Earth even real? Or was she just a voice he made up in his head, a way to fool himself into thinking he had a purpose?

And then it hit him: there was no way to know.

And when you can't know something, you have to choose what to believe. What would he choose?

The cloud of bats vanished, and Taemon could hear the frogs again. The Heart of the Earth would not tamper with free choice. If she gave him a sign, some proof that she existed, then he would have no choice but to believe. She wouldn't do that; she always let him choose. He had to make his choice first. And then he'd be able to see the signs, if there were any.

What would he choose to believe?

A laugh burst from his chest. He had answered his own question. He believed in the Heart of the Earth. He couldn't imagine the world making sense without her. She had spoken to him. She had given him ideas that he never would have come up with on his own, ideas that he sometimes didn't even want to hear. She was real. Of course she was.

Taemon scrambled to his feet and stepped away from the tree. He stretched his arms out on each side, dropped his head back, and looked into the stars. "I choose to believe," he whispered. "I will be a True Son. Please tell me where to go."

And he saw.

In his mind, he saw a place, south of the colony, past the lumber camps, into the Western Forest and close to the smaller mountains south of Mount Deliverance. He had never been there before, but he saw it clearly and understood how to get there.

It was such a relief to know, to have a destination. He didn't care if people didn't like it. He didn't care how much they complained. He knew where to go. He just needed to persuade more people to go with him.

I could use a little help with that, he added.

The wind picked up and ruffled his shirt. He knew somehow that he'd gotten all of the answers he would get tonight. It was time to head for home.

He walked back to the tree to gather his things. Just as he reached for his blanket, a gust of wind picked it up and blew it away from him. In the darkness, Taemon couldn't see where it had gone.

The wind was steady now, flapping at his clothes and stirring his hair. Was there a storm coming? He grabbed his knapsack and hurried to find the trail.

The wind did not let up. If anything, it got stronger. The good thing was that it was at his back, pushing him along the trail. The trees swayed and bent. A good-size tree limb snapped and caromed across his path. This was getting serious. Taemon quickened his step.

The noises were louder, too. The leaves roared as waves of wind crashed into them. A flock of birds flew overhead, squawking with alarm. Then another flock. What in the Great Green Earth was going on?

He stopped and turned to look behind him. An orange glow rimmed the treetops farther up the mountain. The roar wasn't just from the wind. It was from a fire!

Was it the Republik? Had they started the fire?

This is what you asked for, said the Heart of the Earth. **Run!**

Taemon turned and ran. He used his arms to pump. How fast could he run downhill without falling? He found out when he fell. He scrambled to his feet and kept running.

He could feel the heat on his back now. The wind was faster than he was, and the fire would soon overtake him. How had he caused this? He tried to replay his conversation with the Heart of the Earth in his mind, but he couldn't focus his thoughts. Surely he hadn't asked her to set the mountain on fire!

Now he began to see little pockets of flames in front of him, the dry yellow grass bursting into flame before his eyes. His legs and lungs burned with the exertion, but he kept running.

The smoke was getting thicker. He was sucking in heaving breaths now, and the smoke was bad. He tried to pull his shirt up over his nose and mouth, but that slowed him down. He coughed. Something crashed behind him; he didn't dare look.

Something that may have been a bush but was now a ball of flames rolled right into the trail and stopped there. Taemon had to go around. The hem of his pants caught on fire, and he had to stop to beat it out. The heat was sweltering.

He couldn't die now, not when he knew how to lead the people to safety!

He kept running, but he was losing the race against the fire. The flames overtook him. He tried to think of how he could use psi to save himself, but it was hard to think and run and cough and see through the smoke *and* use psi. He drew in a deep breath, and this time he didn't cough. The air was sweet and clean. Smoke billowed and flames leaped all around him, but he could breathe just fine now. And he wasn't burning. He hadn't used any psi at all, but he was safe from the fire. He kept running until the flames ended abruptly. One moment he was surrounded by fire, and the next, he was stepping onto safe ground.

Thank you, he said to the Heart of the Earth.

He looked behind him, still taking deep, clean breaths, and saw where the fire ended. So strange, that it would just stop there. Must be some kind of weird wind pattern on the mountain. Or maybe the colonists had done something to the land that prevented the fire from spreading too far. He would have to ask Hannova about that.

He turned back toward the colony and took slow steps, wishing he still had his water bottle.

As he came closer to the colony, he saw a few people standing on the trail, staring at the fire.

"Don't worry   it's not the Republik," Taemon said.

They turned to him, their eyes wide. Some of them had a hand over their mouth.

Taemon looked down at himself. He must look frightful. His clothes were singed, dotted with little holes in some places. He had streaks of black soot on his arms and probably his face, too.

As he got closer to home, there were more people standing in the trail. They moved out of the way to let Taemon pass, but none of them spoke to him. Had all of these people come to look at the fire? They must have been staying up late, packing their things, and noticed the flames.

Taemon walked a little more quickly. It made him self-conscious, the way everyone was staring at him. He needed to get home, wash up, and change his clothes.

"Taemon!" Someone grabbed him from one side, and he was relieved to see it was Amma. "Are you okay?"

Taemon nodded. "I'm fine. My clothes didn't fare so well, though."

"Oh, thank the Earth, Sea, and Sky. When I saw the flames, I was so scared."

"Cha, I was a little scared myself."

"But now . . ." Amma raised her fist to her mouth. "Taemon, this is exactly what we needed."

"We needed a fire?" Taemon said.

"It's not just a fire; it's a sign." She took his arm again and turned him around. Taemon looked at the flames glowing on the mountainside. Earlier he'd seen only a wall of fire; now he saw the perfect shape of a knife.

Knife. His birth sign.

•   •   •

The next morning, Taemon did his own packing. It took all of twenty minutes. He'd never had many things he could call his own, especially not since he had come to live in the colony: a few clothes, the book Amma had lent him—he wrapped that carefully in a waterproof cloth—a flashlight, a water bottle, a toothbrush, and his scarf. Taemon stood for a moment and tried to think of anything he was forgetting. Drigg had already packed all the food in the house and the camping gear. No use leaving the hauler for the Republik, he'd said.

Taemon looked over his meager possessions. There truly was nothing else he owned, nothing else he needed. He shoved everything in a backpack, swung it over his shoulders, and went to check on Challis and Mam.

As Taemon made his way through the streets, the scene in the colony was chaotic. People everywhere, all of them in a rush. Carts and wagons of every size and shape were scattered about. Some of them had a cow or a mule attached. Parents were trying to keep track of children, children were trying to keep track of dogs, and everyone seemed to be trying to find someone or something before it was time to go.

The confusion and noise nearly overwhelmed him,

but the fact that people were actually preparing to leave, that the argument about whether to go or stay had ended, that part was a relief. And the biggest relief of all was that he now knew where to go. They would head south, following the river as it curved toward the shore. Taemon would lead the people from the colony first, beginning at noon, then Solovar would bring the people from the city behind them.

Taemon tried not to look at the blackened shape of the Knife that smoldered on the mountainside, but his eyes returned to it again and again. Little tendrils of smoke still rose from the symbol, emblazoned like a tattoo on the mountainside for all to see. The sharp edges and the precision of the shape made it thoroughly unnatural. And if the eyes somehow missed it, the smoky smells lingering in the thick summer air would alert the nose.

Most people were preoccupied with their work, but when someone would look up long enough to notice Taemon, they would quickly avert their eyes. They moved away to let him pass, giving him plenty of space, even though the streets were crowded. No one spoke to him, but Taemon caught snatches of their whispers.

" . . . only the True Son could do such a thing."

" . . . just like Nathan . . ."

" . . . going to lead us to safety . ."

" . . . walked straight through the fire . . ."

There were old stories of how Nathan had walked through flames. Taemon was not quite comfortable with people comparing him to a prophet, but if that's what it took to persuade them to follow him, he wouldn't argue.

At Challis's house, Taemon saw about a dozen large bags piled on the porch. Just as he was about to knock, Challis came out with a box in her arms. Taemon took it from her

"Just set it down next to the yarn," Challis said.

"All this is yarn?" Taemon said, looking at the bags that were nearly bursting.

Challis nodded, hands on her hips. "People need soft fuzzy things when they get kicked out of their homes. Good for the spirit. And it's good for your mam to knit, to keep her hands busy."

Taemon set the box on the porch. "I came to see if you needed help."

"That's good of you," Challis said, "but we started packing a few days ago. We're ready."

"You did?" Challis used to see things before they

happened, but that was a long time ago. "Did you know this was going to happen? Did you know all along that we would be leaving the colony?"

Challis laughed. "Drigg told me. A few days ago, he came over and told me we'd be leaving. Told me that your mam and I could ride in the hauler with him, told me to pack as much as I could."

"Drigg," Taemon said.

"No precognition. Just good ol' Drigg."

"How's Mam?" Taemon asked. "What can I do to help?"

"She's fine." Challis opened the door and called inside. "Renda?"

Mam joined them on the porch. "Taemon!" she said, and hugged him. Hugged him! Mam was still new to the powerless ways, and this was his first hug from her. The best hug in the history of hugs.

"I was worried about you!" she said. "We heard about the fire last night. Are you sure you're all right?" She pulled away from him, looked into his eyes, and tried to smooth his hair. He used to hate it when she did that with psi, but now he didn't mind.

Three loud honks made them turn toward the people

gathered in the street. A byrider was trying to make its way through the crowd. "Move aside! Let me through!"

Challis humphed. "A bit of patience would go a long way."

"And common sense," Mam said. "A byrider? With all these people around?"

The driver honked and revved his engine and wove a path through the carts and people. It was a man Taemon recognized, someone who worked for Solovar. He stopped directly in front of Challis's house.

"Taemon Houser! Solovar needs you to come to the city right away."

Taemon stepped forward. "What? He knows I can't come right now."

The driver turned the engine off and stood next to his bike. "It's Yens. He refuses to go."

Mam gasped quietly and raised a hand to her mouth.

The driver continued. "He's gathered a large group of people at the temple. They've been praying all night and they're not going to leave. Solovar is desperate. He needs you to come and talk to Yens. You have to convince him to go."

Mam clutched Taemon's arm. "I'll go with you. We have to talk to Yens."

"We're leaving at noon," Taemon said. "I'm supposed to lead the way. It takes two hours to get to the city. That's not enough time to go and come back."

"We can't just leave him," Mam said.

Taemon knew she was right, but how could he be in two places at once? "Where's Da? Can Da go?"

Ma shook her head. "He's with all the Free Will people. They're on the way here right now. We can't get to him in time."

Taemon turned to the driver. "Wait here for just a minute." He beckoned for Mam and Challis to follow him into the house.

Challis's living room was much the same, except the rug was gone. Taemon sat in an ugly green chair with an even uglier brown doily draped over the back. "I can't be two places at once, and if I go to the city now, it'll mean delaying the departure for everyone. But maybe I can get a message to Yens all the same. Can I have a paper and pencil?" he asked Challis.

He took a moment to choose his words carefully and write them down, then showed them to Mam and Challis.

"The truth is all you can give them," Challis said. "After that, it's up to them."

Studying the words carefully, he drew them in his mind, saw them at once individually and all together. Saw them, felt them, pulled them into himself and held them there. He reached out with psi and let his mind wander across the distance to the city, to the temple. He envisioned the large stones that had tumbled from the temple all those months ago and came to rest on the edge of the gathering place. He knew the very stone that Yens liked to stand on, the tallest one. He saw it clearly in his mind. And he wrote the words there:

Trust in the Heart of the Earth. She will lead you to safety.
Set aside your pride and your own desires. She will protect
Nathan's people and keep all her promises.

For a bit more convincing, Taemon added a Knife symbol at the end of the words. A tiny version of the black shape on the mountainside. *Be it so!*

He released his psi and his breath at the same time. "It's done."

"Let's hope it's enough," Mam whispered.

Taemon stepped onto the porch. The driver was still waiting just below. "I've sent a message. Go back and tell Solovar I've done all I can do."

Skies, he hoped the words on the temple stone were true. He had chosen to believe it, and he did believe it, but he still had no idea how this was going to end.

NAU MILITARY INTEL ADMIN LOGBOOK

> Performance Review completed and filed for Military
Investigator U. Felmark Puster [ID# 229-8831-305]. <

> Recommendation: Promotion of Military Investigator
U. Felmark Puster [ID# 229-8831-305] to Commander. <

> Recommendation: Creation of Special Ops Command Unit
#278 for the express purpose of dealing with Enemies
Demonstrating Psychic Ability [Spec Ops #278/EDPA]. <

> Approval pending. <

17 GEVRI

The invasion of Deliverance was under way. This time,
Gevri was ready. Jix was by his side. He knew this was
what had to be done. For the Republik. For the general.
For the archons. And for himself.

The armies marched through the tunnel two abreast,
the marching songs that Gevri had grown up with echoing
through the mountain itself. The melody and the rhythm
seeped into his heart and made him stronger. This was
not only about settling his argument with Taemon; this
was about bringing justice to the rebels who had followed

Nathan. They had turned their backs on the Republik, not only by deserting it, but also by claiming some of its land for themselves, then sending a famine on their own countrymen.

By the end of the day, all would be made right.

Gevri's unit had the honor of being the first one behind the general's detail. Following him were three more archon units, and after that, six squadrons, each with one hundred soldiers. The noise of all those boots stamping in the tunnel was incredible.

In the darkness of the tunnel, all the soldiers had their helmet lights on. The beams from each marching soldier danced on the smooth rock walls, giving it an almost festive feel.

Two more archon units were working on clearing a path across the mountain for the tanks and the war machines to pass. They wouldn't fit through the tunnel, but they'd find a way through so that Deliverance would be fully prepared for the Nau, whenever they decided to show up.

For now, Gevri needed to check on his archons. Only ten days ago, they were suffering in a Nau prison. They'd gotten excellent attention from the doctors at Kanjai, and they were sturdy little cubs, but Gevri still wanted to make sure they were all right.

"Invert!" He called out the order that told them he was going to change his position from the front of the line to the back. He and Jix stepped aside as the rest of his unit double-timed it past him, then immediately settled back to regular marching pace.

Gevri took his place at the end, behind Cindahad. "How goes it?"

"Great," Cindahad said. "Though I'll be glad to see the sun again."

"You will, soon enough!" He looked at the seven archons marching in front of him, shoulders straight, heads high, feet moving in perfect unity. They looked strong. They looked confident. They looked like they would do whatever Gevri asked of them.

If anything, the time they had spent in the prison had made them stronger, not weaker. There was a oneness among them that had become rock-hard during the tough times in prison. They would follow him into the pits of flame if he asked them to.

That should've made him happy, but it felt like a great stone on his back. Any harm that came to them was because of him. He would not fail them again. They had been through enough.

"Invert!" Gevri called again, then jogged ahead. He and Jix took their places at the front of the line once more.

Nearly an hour later, Gevri saw the sun up ahead. A cheer ran through the ranks.

As they came out of the tunnel, Gevri remembered the last time he had come through it and the humiliation that had followed. Taemon had played his tricks well and taken them all for fools.

Not this time.

The army continued its march on the mountain trails, but they had to switch to single file, which slowed them down a little. The rocky terrain didn't help. Soon they reached the tree line, and the going became a bit easier. Now at least they had soil under their feet instead of scree. They continued down, passing what looked like a deserted mining camp. Up ahead, Gevri caught sight of the walls of the city.

A thrill passed over him. He had never been this far into Deliverance, even when he'd been in Free Will's camp. This was it. This was what he'd been waiting for.

The general called for a different archon unit to take

the lead. Unlike Gevri's archons, these soldiers had only telekinetic dominion, and they were called upon to make a direct path and smooth the way. The unit leader called out his orders, and trees began to fall, crashing with a magnificent splendor, like heralds announcing their presence. This was, after all, no surprise attack.

The rest of the soldiers cheered with each tree that toppled. Gevri and his archons cheered along with them.

A few of those trees were hauled to the river. In a few minutes, the archons had exercised dominion to split the trees and make a crude but sturdy bridge for the soldiers to cross.

Gevri felt just as he had when he walked out of the Nau prison. The army of the Republik was invincible. Nothing could stop them. Nothing could get in their way.

As Gevri crossed the bridge, he looked to either side of him at the tree-lined river. This really was a beautiful place. This land belonged in the Republik once more. All would be restored as it once was.

Something flickered at the corner of his eye. He turned to look at a huge slice of the mountainside that had been burned with fire. What in the gods' names was that? Was that supposed to scare them? Were they trying to send some kind of message? He could tell it was some kind of deliberate shape, but what was it? It looked like a leaf with a top hat on it.

Gevri had to move forward, but he craned his head from time to time to look at the black scar on the mountain.

"What is that?" Saunch asked from behind.

"Well, you know they use a lot of symbols around here," Gevri said. "Probably because most of them aren't smart enough to read."

He meant it to be a joke, but Saunch didn't laugh.

"Anyway, I'm pretty sure I recognize that symbol," Gevri said. "It means, 'Welcome to our home.'"

This time Saunch did laugh. "You're making that up."

"It could be true; you don't know. Let's keep our eyes forward."

And they did. Forward through the woods and hills and meadows that lay between the mountain and the city. They came at the city walls from the northeast, and the general called the army to a halt.

"Lieutenant Sarin," the general called, and Gevri ran forward.

He stood as tall as he could and saluted. "Yes, sir!"

"Use your remote viewers and tell me what is on the other side of that wall."

"Yes, sir!" Gevri called his archons into formation. It wasn't long before they had an answer for the general.

"Sir, on the other side of the wall you will find many small houses. Some of them huts. None of them are very well constructed. As far as we can tell, they are deserted."

The general looked thoughtful. "There are no people whatsoever?"

"None that we have detected, sir," Gevri answered.

"Keep looking. I want to know where the people are."

Gevri huddled with his archons again, then returned to the general.

"Sir, there is a small gathering of people at the city center, by some sort of ruins," Gevri reported. "But most of the city appears to be deserted."

"Bring in the archon units!" boomed the general. "Blast through this wall! We do *not* enter this city through a gate!"

The archon unit blasted a huge opening in the wall, crumbling it to gray-tan dust that moved neatly aside. The soldiers cheered and whooped.

The general was right; bursting through the wall definitely fit the occasion. *There's a symbol for you,* Gevri thought.

The general gave orders for small groups of soldiers to search the houses, just to be sure. The bulk of the army pressed forward to the temple at the center of the city.

The streets were eerily quiet. Not even any barking dogs to greet them.

"They've given up," Saunch said beside him. "They're gone."

Gevri nodded. "But where? Where did they go?" They could be hiding. Did these people know how to hide from remote viewers? Was that even possible? The thought made Gevri uneasy. The Nathanites had been living with psi for a lot longer than the Republik had been exercising dominion. Maybe they had a few more tricks up their sleeves. Wouldn't that be just like them?

"Stay alert," Gevri told his archons. "Remote viewers, I want you to check and double-check. These people have to be somewhere."

"Yes, sir!" came the chorus of replies.

Still, they didn't meet one single person along the way. The soldiers fanned out, but there was no one to attack.

"The only people I can find are the ones at the ruins," Berliott said.

"Same here," Pik said.

Cindahad nodded. "Me, too."

"All right, then," Gevri said. "The ruins it is."

As the army neared the ruins, Gevri heard a humming sound. A rhythmic humming, like some sort of chanting.

And there they were.

About two hundred or so men, women, and children were kneeling in an open space in front of the collapsed building. What had happened here?

The volume of the chanting increased. The people were on their knees with their foreheads pressed to the ground. None of them seemed to take any notice of the soldiers who were surrounding them. Were they in some sort of trance?

The noise seemed to bother Jix, and she paced next to Gevri.

As the soldiers took their positions, Gevri stepped next to his father. "This rubble—did the Nathanites do that?"

The general nodded as he surveyed the scene. "This used to be their temple. Yens—or perhaps Taemon—brought it down on the same day psi was lost."

"How do you know?"

"We had spies here for years. You've met Commander Othaniel?"

Gevri nodded. The man had recently been promoted, skipping ahead several ranks.

"He was one of the priests here," the general said. "Excellent work."

When the soldiers were all in place, the general called out, "Archons, choose your targets!"

Targets? Did he mean people? Gevri stepped close to his father. "We're just going to kill them?" All the excitement he felt in the tunnel had dissipated. It was one thing to kill your enemy in glorious battle. But this wasn't glorious. It wasn't even a battle. This was slaughter.

The general gave him a flat look that said, *Must we go through this again?*

"I think we should take them as prisoners," Gevri offered. "Then find the rest of them, wherever they're hiding, and try to —"

"We'll hunt them down easily enough," the general said. "A group that large can't cover its tracks."

General Sarin waved to the leader of one of the archon units, who came running over. "Lieutenant Sarin has requested that we take prisoners. But I wish to take only one." The general pointed to the young man in the scarlet robes kneeling on the tallest stone. "Him."

"And the others?"

"Destroy them."

NAU MILITARY INTEL ADMIN LOGBOOK

> Approval granted for the creation of Special Ops
Command Unit #278 for dealing with Enemies Demonstrating
Psychic Ability. Commander U. Felmark Puster [ID#
229-8831-305] assigned as officer in charge. Effective
immediately. <

> Spec Ops Command Unit #278 assigned to Foreign Sector
#083 [aka The Republik]. Priority level: 99H. <

18 TAEMON

Taemon rode in the cab of the hauler with Drigg. They were inching along so that they didn't get too far ahead of the people who were walking, which was most everyone else. A few people had carts or wagons pulled by mules, a few more were on horseback, but all in all, the great evacuation of Deliverance moved slowly.

Drigg had left the benches in the back of the hauler and had older and infirm people riding in the back, Challis and Mam included. He had also lowered the ceiling and put rails on top of the hauler, which gave him a place to strap down all his cargo. The hauler was quite an amazing display of versatility, as it was one of the few larger vehicles used for transportation in the colony. And Drigg had made the most of it.

"How far do you think we'll be able to drive on this road?" Drigg asked.

"Until we cross the river and reach the fishing camp, where the road ends. Then we'll have to travel on foot and head west along the coast."

"West?" Drigg said.

"West." Luckily Drigg didn't press for any more details, because that was everything Taemon knew. He'd seen the place they needed to go, and he was sure he could find it, but after that, he had no idea what would happen. He didn't know the exact number of people in his group—sickness and hunger had taken their toll in the months since the Fall—but he knew there were still thousands of people following him. They couldn't very well hide from the army of the Republik.

Solovar rode up next to the hauler on his horse. "How much longer today?"

"We made almost ten miles yesterday," Taemon said. "If we can do twelve miles today, we should be able to get across the river. We can camp by the fishing huts tonight."

"All right, I'll spread the word," Solovar said, and started to turn his horse away.

"Wait," Taemon called. "Any news about Yens?" He'd asked Solovar to search the crowd for him, but no one had seen him. In all the confusion of getting such a large group of people on the road, there were conflicting reports about the people who had gathered at the temple.

"Nothing yet, but I'll keep looking." Solovar led his horse back toward the people.

Taemon felt a pang of guilt. He should be walking with the people, not riding in the hauler with the infirm. They had agreed that he would ride so he could save his strength in case he had to use psi, but it was their third day on the road, and he just didn't feel right about it anymore. "I think I'll walk for a while," he told Drigg.

Drigg stopped the hauler and turned to Taemon. "Are you sure?"

Taemon nodded and climbed out.

Drigg moved the truck along at a crawl, and Taemon walked beside it. It felt good to stretch his legs.

Amma jogged up to him a few minutes later. "I thought you were going to ride."

Taemon shrugged. "Just felt like walking for a while. Where's your family?"

Amma turned and pointed behind her. "My mam's right there, near the front of the line. Da wants us there so he can find us easily."

Taemon turned and saw Amma's mother walking next to a small cart pulled by a mule. She waved at him, and he waved back. Amma's father and her two brothers were on horseback, riding up and down the line of people, checking on everyone and helping people with problems.

"There's something I've been meaning to tell you," Taemon said. "When I was looking for Gevri in Kanjai, I found him in a room filled with crates of books. I don't know for sure, but my guess is that they're from your library. I'm sure I can find the room again."

Amma perked up at this news, but then her face fell and she sighed. "How likely are we to ever get to Kanjai again, though? I mean, if we need to rebuild Deliverance, that could take years, right? Somehow I doubt getting the books will be anyone's priority."

"Where'd you get the idea that we were going to rebuild?" Taemon asked.

"Isn't that the plan?" Amma asked. "We can't return to Deliverance as long as war rages between the Republik and the Nau. Besides, when Solovar rode by, he told us we were going to the fishing huts, so everyone assumes that's where we'll be settling, since there's nothing past that except the ocean."

Taemon smiled and bumped Amma with his shoulder. It threw her off balance a little.

"Hey, what was that for?"

"That was for you, Water Girl. I thought you'd like the ocean."

"I love the ocean. But I'm wondering if I'll ever see my home again."

"I'm wondering, too," Taemon admitted.

"But, hey, I guess it's good we know where the books are. Maybe someday . . ."

"Cha," Taemon said. "Maybe someday."

They walked in silence for a little longer. Clouds passed over the sun and threw shadows across the road in front of them. "I'm really, really sorry about all this," Taemon said.

"All what?" Amma asked.

Taemon threw his arms wide. "The books, the library, The Fall, the war, the Republik, the Nau. Everything!"

"So now the war is your fault?" Amma said. "As I recall, the war between the Republik and the Nau has been going on for decades. I'm pretty sure you didn't start it."

"No, but it's because of me that we're in the middle of it."

Amma didn't say anything at first. When Taemon turned to look at her, she was staring blankly at the road ahead. "You know what I think? I think we would have been in the middle of it no matter what."

"Well, I'm going to find a way to get us out of it. Leaving Deliverance was just the first step," Taemon said. He was glad Amma didn't ask him what the next steps were. But maybe that was because she sensed that he didn't actually know.

The afternoon wore on, and the refugees from Deliverance plodded onward. The hauler and the front of the line made it to the fishing huts just before dark, which was fortunate. It would take a couple more hours for everyone to pour in. There were only a few huts, which went to the elderly and the infirm, and everyone else camped outside.

Being this close to the river was helpful. At least they had a fresh water supply.

Mam and Challis were fixing their bedrolls in the back of the hauler, and Taemon was helping Drigg set up the tent where the men would sleep. Da would be joining them later that evening. He was overseeing the people from Free Will.

When a horse came galloping up to him, Taemon thought it would be Da, but it was Amma's da, followed by one of her brothers, also on horseback. Riding behind Rhody was a figure wrapped in a gray blanket.

Mr. Parvel reined in his horse and dismounted. "We have news. The army of the Republik has reached the city. They killed all the people who were gathered at the temple."

Taemon took a quick breath. "How many?"

"We're not sure," Mr. Parvel said. "More than a hundred."

Taemon closed his eyes. More than a hundred. He had tried to tell them. He had done everything he could. Hadn't he? "Was Yens with them?"

Mr. Parvel didn't answer at first, and Taemon feared the worst.

"He's right here," Mr. Parvel said, pulling Rhody's passenger down from the horse.

The blanket slipped off one shoulder, revealing the rumpled and torn red silk tunic. Yens stood before Taemon, slumped and dazed.

Taemon fought the urge to hug his brother. Hugging would be foreign to Yens—and even if it wasn't, they had never had that kind of relationship. But Skies, was he glad to see his brother alive—despite all their differences. "What happened?"

Yens slowly lifted his head, blinked, and stared at Taemon with an unfocused gaze. "It was horrible," he whispered. "I didn't . . . I couldn't . . ."

"He told us that they killed everyone in the gathering place," Mr. Parvel said with an iron-cold tone. "When he realized what was happening, he fell down and pretended to be dead. When the army left, he snuck away. We found him wandering in the woods, making a racket."

Taemon couldn't tell if Rhody and Mr. Parvel doubted Yens's story or if they resented the fact that he out of everyone survived. After all, if it hadn't been for Yens, those one hundred men, women, and children wouldn't have been there in the first place.

Still, Yens was alive, and that was the first good news Taemon had heard in a long time. "Let me take him to Mam," Taemon said. "Then we'll talk."

Taemon put one arm around Yens and led him to the hauler. "Look who's here," he said, hoping he sounded cheerful. He helped Yens into the hauler, where Mam and Challis embraced him—despite his flinching—and gave him food and water. Taemon walked back to Mr. Parvel and Rhody.

"You two doubt his story?"

"Unfortunately, I believe the killing part is true," Mr. Parvel said. "But it's hard to believe he just snuck away like that."

"I think they sent him here," Rhody said. "Maybe turned him loose on purpose to see if he would lead them right to us."

Taemon frowned. "If that's true, then he did lead them right to us."

"Cha," Rhody said.

"How many people know about this?" Taemon asked.

"No one else, at least not yet," Mr. Parvel said. "We brought him straight to you. But there are plenty of people worried about those who stayed behind."

Taemon nodded. "Did you see anything for yourself? The army? The . . . bodies?"

"No. We couldn't get that close." Mr. Parvel looked away.

"We saw the wall where they broke into the city," Rhody said. "We saw their tracks."

"What is the army doing now?"

"There are lights in some of the houses of the city," Rhody said, a hard look on his face. "Plenty of hollering and laughing. They're whooping it up."

"We think they'll stay the night there," added Mr. Parvel. "Tomorrow they'll be on our tails, for sure."

"We'll have to leave at first light," Taemon said. "We'll have to move fast."

Rhody looked at him like he was klonkers. "Where can we go from here?"

"We're turning west tomorrow," Taemon said with as much confidence as he could manage.

"West? Into the mountains?" Rhody asked.

"That's right."

Mr. Parvel rubbed the stubble on his cheeks. "I hate to say this, Taemon, but we're in the worst possible place we could be. We've gone as far south as we can go, right up to the ocean. If we go east, that takes us closer to the city. We can't go north, because that takes us back to the colony, where they'll surely find us."

"Which is why we're going west," Taemon said.

"We can only go a few miles," Rhody said. "Then our backs are up against the mountain. You're not planning to go over the mountain, are you? Because we won't make it. It's much too steep here, and we're not climbers. Well, me and Abson are, but nobody else."

Taemon didn't have an answer for that.

"He's right, Taemon," Mr. Parvel said. "We'll never get this mob across that mountain range. This far west, there are no passes. No secret tunnels. Nothing but sheer, rocky cliffs that stretch out into the ocean."

That sounded exactly like the place he'd seen, the place the Heart of the Earth had shown him. "Yes, that's where we're going."

A look of panic swept over Rhody's face. "Then you're backing us into a corner," he whispered.

"It sure seems that way to me," Mr. Parvel added.

"I know what it seems," Taemon said. "But this is the only way it will work out. You need to trust me on this."

Mr. Parvel and Rhody exchanged grim looks.

"Well, at least no one can sneak up on us from behind," Mr. Parvel said. "We're just going to have to plant ourselves in our little corner and fight like the blazes."

"More like go out in a blaze of glory," Rhody muttered.

"This is the only way it will work, believe me," Taemon repeated, but Rhody just shook his head and walked away. Mr. Parvel followed.

Taemon returned to help with the tent, but Drigg had already finished assembling it.

Another horse galloped up, and this time it *was* Da. Taemon helped him take care of the horse, and the two of them went to see how Yens was doing. As Taemon sat in the back of the hauler with Challis, Mam, Da, and Yens, he realized that for the first time in two years, his family was all together.

If I have to go out in a blaze of glory, thought Taemon, *this is what I would choose for my last night.*

NAU MILITARY INTEL ADMIN LOGBOOK

> Outpost Observation Unit Report, Foreign Sector #083:
Massive movements of Republik military units in addition
to unidentified foreign personnel. Recommendation: Raise
status alert to RED. <

> Recommendation approved. <

> Direct Communication from Commander U. Felmark Puster
[ID# 229-8831-305]: Emergency Request for Air Support,
classifications VN32 and VJ27. <

> Emergency Request approved. <

19 GEVRI

The army of the Republik was enjoying a raucous night
of celebrating in the Nathanites' abandoned houses, but
Gevri didn't feel like celebrating. What he'd seen at the
temple had left him feeling hollow. He walked slowly, his
hand reaching out for Jix now and then.

What did you expect? he asked himself. *Tea and
samkins? It's a war. There will be casualties.* Still, he hadn't
expected anything like that, not at all. He'd expected
a noble clash of warrior against warrior, a battle of wits

and strength and endurance. Those people never fought back at all. Most of them didn't even lift their heads from prayer.

"They made a choice," his father had said. "They chose to die."

Gevri just couldn't believe that. And even if it was true, did that make it right to kill them in such a dishonorable way?

Jix butted her head against Gevri's leg.

"What is it?" Gevri looked up and saw that he'd led his archons into a dead-end street, a place that looked like it had once been a nice neighborhood but had fallen into shambles. From a distance, he heard whoops, crashes, and bursts of wild laughter. The other units were having fun. The general *had* given them free run of whatever they could find, but Gevri didn't want his young soldiers mixing with the older men and women who were entertaining themselves by ransacking houses.

"Pair up and look for food," Gevri said. "Then meet me at the big house on the end of the street."

There was so little food in these houses. His unit had to go inside at least ten houses before they'd found enough food to put together a meal. Everything seemed broken or patched together or repurposed. This street had the look of a place that had once known wealth and prestige but had fallen into neglect and poverty. They couldn't even get the water to come out of the faucets. The lights were just about the only thing that worked.

Stop it, Gevri told himself. *Don't feel sorry for them. They brought this on themselves.* Why was he having all these second thoughts? Everything had felt so right on the march over here. He tried to summon those feelings of certainty, but it was becoming impossible. What were his options now? He couldn't let his father down, not again. He couldn't desert or quit or change his mind. He'd chosen this path; now he had to walk it.

They scraped together a meal, then he let the archons play cards until Pik started losing his temper. At that point, they all bedded down for the night. But Gevri lay awake for hours, reliving the horror he'd seen. Jix nuzzled his hand, but even that didn't help him sleep.

The next day, the Republikite army was on the move again. Despite the celebrations that stretched into the late hours, they'd gotten an early start. Gevri, along with his archons and Jix, were near the front, as usual, and Gevri was in the lead. From all the reports, the Nathanites had a two-day lead on them, but everyone knew a trained army could move much faster than a bunch of slow civilians. They'd catch up to them soon enough. There was no place for them to run. The tunnel was guarded heavily, and Gevri was pretty sure Taemon wasn't going to send all those folks over the mountain on kites.

They were moving west now on a fairly nice road. West to the river, then south toward the ocean. That's what the scouts had told them. After two solid hours of marching, someone up ahead called for a halt. Gevri led his group under a tree.

"Eat some travel rations," Gevri told his unit. They hadn't found enough food for a decent breakfast. "And drink water." He poured some water for Jix to drink.

"I still don't get it," Saunch said. "Why do we have to follow them? Why can't we just let them go?"

Gevri chewed his stale, dense travel bar and had to take two swallows of water before he could talk—it was that dry. "We can't risk it," Gevri said, even though he'd had similar thoughts. He was a leader, and he needed to act like it. "We can't have them just traipsing around out there."

"Why not?" Saunch asked.

Gevri looked Saunch in the eye. "We've talked about this before. We can't run the risk of them becoming allies to the Nau."

The archons were silent. Probably because their travel bars were just as dry and dense as his.

Gevri continued, "Look, you were in on the planning meetings. Remember the plan? When we catch up to them, the general is going to give them one more chance to join us. And if they don't, well, then they have made their choice."

Jix lifted her head with a sudden alertness.

"Hold on," Berliott said. "I'm picking up on something else. There's something . . . in the mountain." Her voice had a soft, dreamy tone.

Gevri shook her shoulder. "Berliott? Don't overextend. Break the connection. Now!"

She shuddered, then looked at Gevri. The clarity and sharpness in her eyes made Gevri sigh with relief. She had broken the connection in time.

"What did you see?"

"Republik war machines. Blasting and drilling their way through the mountains," Berliott said. "Followed by a line of tanks."

"Are you sure?" Gevri asked.

"Yes, sir."

The general had never shared that part of the plan. But Gevri wouldn't put it past him. His father loved dramatic entrances, and shocking the Nathanites into submission with tanks and war machines certainly fit his style.

"Cindahad and Pik, I want you to take turns with Berliott. Rotate every fifteen minutes. Use your remote viewing and keep me informed of the war machines' progress. Along with anything else you see. But be careful! Do not overextend. I can't afford to lose any of you. Understood?"

"Yes, sir!" they replied in unison.

Gevri took another drink of water but had trouble swallowing. His throat felt tight. *Gods, let Taemon have the sense to surrender. If not, this is going to be a bloodbath.*

When he reached out to stroke Jix, her neck muscles felt rigid. She was as tense as Gevri.

NAU MILITARY INTEL ADMIN LOGBOOK

> Direct Communication from Commander U. Felmark Puster
[ID# 229-8831-305]: Confirmed use of psychic powers in
acts of aggression. Recommendation: Elimination of all
enemy personnel manifesting aberrant psychic ability. <

> Recommendation approved. <

20 TAEMON

Breakfast was a handful of dried fruit and some crackers. Challis brought Taemon and Yens steaming cups of her herbal tea. Yens had been quiet so far this morning, which was more unsettling than his usual arrogant comments.

Challis handed each of the boys a warm mug, then sat on a folding stool next to Taemon. "I noticed you haven't used any psi at all on this trip. Not that I could tell, anyway."

Taemon took a sip, then shook his head. "I'll only use it when I absolutely have to."

Yens looked up from his mug with wild eyes. "You have to use it when the army catches us, Tae. You have to. You cannot let them do what they did yesterday. They slaughtered every one of those people. They—" His voice faltered, and he lowered his head to his mug again.

Mam walked over and rubbed his back. "Taemon will do the right thing."

Taemon shoved a few dried blueberries into his mouth and tried not to think about it.

Challis cleared her throat. "I just want to say one more thing. The Heart of the Earth left you with psi for a reason. Whatever you have to do, if you need psi to do it, then don't be afraid to use it."

Before they even broke up camp, Mr. Parvel rode in with news. "Abson and Rhody rode out early this morning. The Republikites are already moving this way."

"On foot?" Taemon asked.

"On foot," Mr. Parvel confirmed. "But marching quickly. Much more quickly than we can move. They'll overtake us later today."

"Tell everyone to get moving," Taemon said. "We have to make it to the cliffs today."

As the cliffs loomed nearer and nearer, Taemon felt his nerves beginning to unravel. He had been so focused on getting to the cliffs that he hadn't spent much time thinking about what came next. How were these defenseless people meant to ward off the Republikite army? Would the Heart of the Earth tell him what to do once they reached the cliffs, or would he be left to figure it out on his own?

The gray-white cliffs seemed to grow taller, and Taemon began to feel smaller. How could he dare hope to live through this, let alone be victorious?

Finally, as the afternoon wore on, the group reached the cliffs, and the Parvels began directing the elderly, the infirm, and the children toward the back, close to the water, while the carts, wagons, and anyone willing to fight moved into position to meet the army that would surely come.

Where was Amma? When Taemon asked after her, he learned that her father had given her his horse to care for.

Taemon suspected it was Mr. Parvel's way of making sure she stayed near the rear.

As the people of Deliverance drew together in a tight bunch, Taemon fought to focus his thoughts. He needed to clear his head, to be open to messages from the Heart of the Earth. He needed to step away from the crowd for a moment.

Yens followed him.

"Yens, I need to be alone right now," Taemon said.

"No, I'm staying with you."

Taemon frowned. Was this Yens's idea of loyalty? That was hard to swallow. More likely, Yens was trying to save his own skin. "Look, don't think I can protect you. They'll try to kill me first, you know."

"Well, then, I'll be your bodyguard. Who's better suited for that job than a big brother?"

Taemon laughed. He wanted to remind Yens of at least three instances when Yens had tried to kill him. But that was in the past. Eons ago. "I mean it," he said. "I need a few minutes to think."

"Listen to me, Taemon. I was at the temple. I saw what they did. You *cannot* let that happen again."

"We've already had this conversation. I know what you're going to say, Yens, and—"

"You're going to have to kill the general," Yens said. "Skies, just kill the whole army. You could do it. You could do it right now if you wanted to. Just reach out and—" Yens made a strangling motion with his hands.

"Stop it, Yens."

"Couldn't you?" Yens yelled.

"I could. But how is that different from what the soldiers did at the temple yesterday?"

Yens scowled. "It's not the same. Not at all."

"It feels the same to me," Taemon said. "Do you know the first time I wanted to kill someone with psi? It was you, Yens. I almost killed you, my own brother. That day, that very hour, I promised myself I would never kill you or anyone else with psi. I just can't do it."

Yens's shoulders sagged. "But you'll stand by and watch other people get killed."

"I can't control what other people do. I can only control what I do."

Yens locked eyes with him, and in that moment, Taemon wanted more than anything to simply understand Yens. He focused on Yens's face, tried to read his expression, tried to look deeper. He slid so easily into clairvoyance; he didn't even remember summoning psi. This time, he wasn't looking inside an engine or a lock. He was looking inside his brother, looking into the very core of what made him tick. Not his bones and muscles this time, but his emotions. And those emotions were a tangled web of many opposing desires.

Yens was torn in two directions right now. On one hand, he envied Taemon's power to save the lives of all the people of Deliverance. The fact that Taemon had that power instead of he—it was almost more than he could bear. But he also craved the love and acceptance of his family. And he felt guilt. So much guilt wrapped around everything.

Taemon reached out and put his arm around Yens.

It seemed to startle him at first, but then he leaned into Taemon. His shoulders shook. "All those people stayed because of me. They died because of me."

"You didn't kill them," Taemon said. "The soldiers did."

Even as Taemon heard the consoling words leave his mouth, he understood the feeling of being crushed by guilt. If he had done what Yens had, he would feel just as guilty as his brother. How many times had Taemon felt the weight of what he'd done to the people of Deliverance? He'd taken away psi, stripped them of the ability to defend themselves. All he was trying to do was follow the Heart of the Earth. He could not let himself crumble under these feelings of guilt and despair. He had to keep trying to the very end.

The tenderness ended the moment Taemon heard the rolling thunder of hundreds of marching feet.

The army of the Republik had arrived.

21 GEVRI

Gevri watched his father shouting orders over his radio.

"I want them surrounded!" he said. "Hem them in from the shoreline all the way to the cliffs! No way out!"

The general was in his glory. This was his moment. Gevri wondered what his own role in this battle was going to be. Much of that depended on how Taemon reacted to being trapped in a corner. So far, the only thing his father had asked him to do with dominion was to set up the command tent. He stood in the tent now, waiting for the general to give him his next orders after he was done talking to one of his commanders on the radio. Jix waited outside. The general did not allow her inside his tent.

"Priority number one is to get the perimeter set up. After that, start setting up camps. We'll be here at least one night. Maybe more." He paused, and Gevri heard the faint squawks of the person on the other end of the call. "It doesn't matter how long we have to wait. The Nathanites aren't going anywhere." Another pause. "We've taken all that into account. I have a psi blocker hidden nearby."

So Taemon wouldn't be able to use psi. Gevri wasn't sure how he felt about that. In some ways, it was a relief. In other ways, he wished for a fair fight.

"We can stall," said the general. "It will make us look . . . merciful." He chuckled, then ended the transmission.

"We're stalling?" Gevri said "Why, sir?"

The general gathered up the papers on the table and shoved them in a file. "We're waiting for one more guest at our little party."

"Sir, if it's the war machines you're waiting for, my remote viewers tell me they should be here within the hour," Gevri said.

The general took a moment to respond, and Gevri

thought he saw a hint of surprise in his father's eyes. Gevri felt certain he hadn't expected the remote viewers to sense the war machines.

"Perfect," said the general, returning Gevri's gaze with a chilling smile.

Gevri couldn't remain silent. "Sir, what is the point of a bloodbath? These people are unarmed. They have no power. Taemon is the only one we should be fighting."

The general stepped closer, within an inch of Gevri's face. "Control your emotions, soldier." He spoke each word with a quiet fierceness

Gevri steeled himself. He stood his ground, stared straight ahead, but without focusing on his father's face. He imagined he was looking through his father and focused instead on the wall of the tent.

"There will be no bloodbath. All of this has been calculated from the beginning. A vast invading army, the killings at the temple, the war machines bursting from the mountain. Only a great fool would continue to resist. The Nathanites will capitulate. They will join us."

Gevri lifted his chin. "And if Taemon calls your bluff? What then?"

"I never bluff." The general tugged at the hem of his

jacket, relaxed his shoulders, and headed toward the door of the tent.

"What do you want me to do, sir?" Gevri asked as he followed.

"I want you with me. You and your unit."

"Yes, sir." As they left the tent, Jix fell into place beside Gevri, and the other archons formed up behind.

They followed the general to the front lines, where the soldiers had set up barricades. Gevri's father strode confidently, right up behind the soldiers who were kneeling behind the barricade. "At ease, men. Our enemy doesn't have one bullet between the lot of them."

The soldiers laughed and relaxed their stance.

The general even went so far as to pat one of them on the shoulder. "I'm just going to have a chat with them. You men keep your eyes sharp and tell me if you see anything unusual. Lieutenant Sarin?" The general looked over his shoulder. "I want you right next to me. Position your archons nearby."

"Yes, sir," Gevri answered, and motioned for his archons to take on the formations they'd practiced. When he saw that they were in position, he rested one hand on

Jix's back, then turned to face the Nathanites, searching for Taemon in the crowd.

The Nathanites had tried to set up their own barrier, made up of wagons and carts that looked about a hundred years old. They'd even propped up sacks of grain and bags of fruit to fill in some of the gaps. The barricade didn't even reach all the way to the beach. The army would have no trouble getting through. It was like fighting a bunch of peasants.

"Lieutenant Sarin, you will amplify my voice as I speak. Ready?"

"Ready, sir."

The general took a deep breath, which was Gevri's signal to amplify his voice.

"Taemon Houser! Yens Houser! Come forward."

Gevri exercised dominion to make the general's voice boom and echo from the cliffs. It was quite impressive, even for dominion.

Then Gevri saw him. With his brother behind him, Taemon stepped out in front of the wagons, holding his arms out at his sides, palms forward. The sign of peace.

"I ask you to leave us in peace," Taemon said,

amplifying his own voice. Apparently the general hadn't yet turned on the psi blocker. "We've done nothing to threaten you."

"You have refused to form an alliance with us," the general said. "That is threat enough."

"We will not take part in this war. To do so would dishonor Nathan and all his teachings. He refused to use his powers for destruction, and we will follow him." Taemon stood tall as he spoke.

He has guts, Gevri said to Jix. *I have to give him that.*

The jaguar chuffed in agreement.

Taemon continued. "We will not ally with you, nor will we ally with the Nau nations. I promise you that."

A promise from a Nathanite was no promise at all— Gevri knew that better than anyone.

"The risk is too great," the general said. "If you will not be our ally, we must destroy you. So I am asking you one more time, Taemon Houser: Will you align yourself with the Republik and pledge yourself and your people to fight with us to defeat the Nau?" The general knew how to make his voice dramatic, and Gevri added just the right volume and tones to make it sound really impressive. The Republik soldiers let out a cheer.

The cheer died down, but Taemon had not yet responded. He seemed to be listening to the air itself.

"The choice is yours, Taemon. Join with us, fight with us, share in our victory, or be destroyed."

Taemon was staring right at the general, but he wasn't saying anything. What was he doing? Gevri's father seemed content to let the silence linger, and every second made Gevri more nervous.

"General," whispered Gevri, "should we activate the psi blocker?"

"Not yet." He signaled for Gevri to amplify his voice again. "What say you, Taemon? Do you wish to live? Or do you wish to die?"

After another moment of silence, Taemon finally found his voice. "If you would choose to slaughter an innocent people rather than trust in our ability to be true to our word, then so be it."

A murmur rippled through the Republikite army. Taemon was *daring* the general to kill them all. Gevri felt sick; how could Taemon underestimate his father so drastically?

Taemon's response seemed to catch the general off guard as well, though he struggled to hide his surprise.

"So be it!" the general boomed. "We will do you the courtesy of giving you one last night together. Say your good-byes; make whatever preparations you must. But at first light, know that your fates will all be sealed."

A still moment passed, heavy with tension.

Thunder rumbled in the distance, and it seemed to bother Jix. She paced in a tight circle, then sat down again.

"Maintain your positions!" the general called to his soldiers. With that, he turned and strode toward his tent.

Gevri followed the general and motioned for his unit to do the same. He addressed his father in a quiet voice. "Sir—"

The general held up his hand for silence. "Do not doubt me. Their resolve will crumble by morning. We must be strong."

Another commander of an archon unit approached. "Sir, should I have the archon units dismantle the barricade?"

"No, Commander. The barricade will make no difference."

"Sir, what about the psi blocker? Should we activate it now?"

"Not yet," the general said without breaking his stride.

"Taemon won't use psi to attack soldiers. We don't need the psi blocker until the heavy equipment gets here."

As though he'd planned it, a rumbling sound shook the earth just then.

Jix growled.

Mumbled sounds of confusion came from the soldiers.

Gevri stopped and turned toward the mountains. The rumbling grew louder, and the cliffs themselves seemed to tremble. "Is that what I think it is?" he said to Berliott.

She nodded.

The rumble became a mighty crescendo, ending with an explosion. Part of the mountain had crumbled at its base. Boulders and rocks that had broken free from the mountain rolled to the sides, and a Republik war machine surged through the hole in the mountain. The soldiers greeted it with a hearty cheer, and Jix released a fitting roar.

Through the new hole in the mountain rolled war machine after war machine, tanks, and supply trucks, all taking positions behind the troops.

The general had stopped to watch as well. He beamed and turned to the archon commander. "Now we will activate the psi blocker."

Gevri searched out Taemon across the field and watched his face. Taemon wore a look of horror as he watched the military vehicles pouring out of the belly of the mountain. When Taemon gripped the sides of his head, Gevri knew the psi blocker was on full blast.

Accept it, Taemon. You are defeated.

22 TAEMON

Taemon doubled over, bracing his hands on his knees. A blast of pain stabbed like a knife between his eyes. General Sarin must have planted a psi blocker somewhere. It was close, very close. And it was turned up full blast.

Yens had a grip on his shoulders. "We have to do something. They're going to kill everyone!"

"I . . . can't . . ." Taemon mumbled.

"Amma!" Yens yelled. "What's going on?"

She came. Taemon felt a gentle hand on his back and caught the familiar honey scent of her hair. "What is it?"

"Psi blocker," Taemon managed to say through clenched teeth. "Really close."

"Can you tell where it is?" Amma said.

Taemon tried to think, but his brain wasn't cooperating. Where? Where was that horrid signal coming from? He forced himself to stand up straight, his eyes still shut tight. "Let me think for a minute."

"Give him some space, Yens," Amma said. "The attack isn't till the morning."

"But we have to do something!" Yens said. "We have to—"

"Give him some space, Yens." Amma was more forceful this time.

Yens hesitated. "All right, but I'll be close by. Don't take too long."

The pain began to subside a bit, and Taemon opened his eyes. Yens was gone.

"Can you use psi?" Amma asked.

Taemon started to shake his head, but thought better of it. The pain had settled into an ache inside his skull. "No."

"What would you like to do now?"

"I'd like to take apart those war machines," Taemon said, "but that's not an option."

"Just stay here," Amma said. "I'll find Hannova and Solovar and all the others. There has to be something we can do besides sit here and wait for the attack."

"Okay." Taemon sat down to wait, rubbing his temples.

One by one, the leaders of Deliverance arrived. Solovar first, then Mam and Da, Challis, Drigg, and Hannova.

"It can't end like this," Solovar said.

"The Heart of the Earth won't desert us," Da said.

"Taemon," said Challis, "you're going to have to use psi."

"He won't do it, even if he could." Yens was back. "I think we should do what the general wants. Anything is better than everyone dying."

"There has to be another way," Hannova said.

Taemon sat on the ground, cradling his head in his hands. The pain had worsened. "We need to find that psi blocker."

"What does that matter if you won't use psi anyway?" Yens said.

"I will use it," Taemon said. "I just won't kill with it."

Yens huffed. "And you expect to defeat an army?"

"What does the device look like?" Da asked. "How big is it?"

Taemon's head throbbed. It was a struggle just to follow the conversation. "It's just a small device. I don't understand how the general got the device close enough to work on me. He can't possibly have a spy among our people, not anymore. And he couldn't have known that we were headed to these cliffs. Amma, do you have any ideas?"

When she didn't answer, Taemon looked up. The sunlight was fading. Was it that late already?

He scanned the faces clustered around him, but Amma wasn't there. "Where's Amma?"

"She borrowed my horse to gather everyone for the meeting," Rhody said. "There's probably someone she couldn't find."

"Who?" Taemon said. "Everyone in the council is here." Everyone but Amma.

NAU MILITARY INTEL ADMIN LOGBOOK

> Direct Communication from Commander U. Felmark Puster
[ID# 229-0831-305]. Emergency Request for permission to
engage the enemy. <

> Permission granted. <

23 GEVRI

Behind the ridge that the Republikite army occupied,
Gevri knelt beside Jix. He and half his unit had been
assigned to the front line to keep watch. The other half
were resting and would take the next rotation. It was
nearly sunset, and a patchy mist had begun to form over
the wild grass. Gevri stared at the wagons and carts that
the Nathanites had lined up as a barricade. What was
going on over there? Were they preparing to fight? Or preparing to die?

A dark shape appeared in the mist.

"Sir? It's a horse."

"I see it, soldier," Gevri answered. "Hold your fire."

The horse was making its way slowly, and its rider held a white cloth over her head. It was Amma.

"I repeat, hold your fire." Gevri rose and climbed over the ridge, Jix at his side.

"I'm unarmed," Amma called out.

"Amma, you shouldn't be here," Gevri said.

She brought the horse to a halt but didn't dismount. The horse eyed Jix with a wild stare, twitching its tail and nickering.

"Hello, Jix," she said. "And Gevri."

He couldn't quite read the tone of her voice when she said his name. It wasn't contempt, exactly. Something closer to disappointment.

She patted the horse's neck. "It's okay. Jix won't hurt you."

"You should go back," Gevri said. "And try to talk some sense into Taemon."

"There's something you need to know." Amma reached down to hand him something.

Gevri hesitated. Was this some kind of trick? While Taemon had been the one who had lied to Gevri during the time he'd traveled with the two of them, Amma had gone along with it. As much as he wanted to trust her, she was still a Nathanite.

"Take it." She thrust the package at him.

Against his better judgment, he stepped forward, took the package from her, and pulled back the leather wrapped around it. "An old book?"

"I marked the place you need to read," she said. "The past isn't what you thought. It isn't what we thought, either."

The horse whinnied and stamped nervously.

"Read it. Get your da to read it. There's a peaceful way out of this."

"Lieutenant Sarin," called one of the soldiers, "do you require assistance?"

Gevri locked eyes with Amma. He saw no fear, no anger. He saw trust.

"Negative," Gevri called over his shoulder. When he turned back to Amma, she was leading the horse back to the Nathanites.

Two hours later, Gevri was sitting in the general's tent. He was off duty for this rotation and had left Saunch in charge of the archon special unit.

"You've read what it says," Gevri said, gesturing toward the ancient book that lay on the table between him and his father. "How can you say it doesn't matter? Nathan didn't cause the famine or take land from the Republik out of malice. He did it because he thought it was the only way to save the Republik from the Nau."

The general tapped the book's cover with his fingers. "Can you vouch for the authenticity of this book?"

"No, of course not."

"That's right," the general said. "No one can. This is most likely one of their clever tricks, manufactured to suit their purpose."

Gevri frowned. "How could they manufacture a book like this? That technology no longer exists."

"The boy has psi," the general said. "It's certainly possible for him to produce something like this."

Gevri opened the book, then leaned down to examine it. "It even smells old. I believe it's real."

"You believe it because you choose to believe it, not because of any real evidence."

Gevri set the book down slowly and ran his hand down its spine. "All right, then. I'm choosing to believe it. And why not? It's a way to end this conflict peacefully. Why shouldn't we make that choice?"

The general took a long breath. "That fool of a boy tries to force my hand with this book and you expect me to back down?"

"The book changes everything, Father. It gives you a way out. You can announce that new information has come to light. You can explain that—"

"I will explain nothing!" Gevri's father gripped the edge of the table and leaned forward. "I don't understand you. I thought you'd finally gotten over the softness of your childhood. You're a man now, son. A man doesn't back down from the tough choices."

Gevri could feel a slow burn rising in his blood. After witnessing the slaughter at the temple two days ago, he could not take part in anything like that again. How could his father do such things? Gevri would never be the man his father wished him to be. And he no longer wanted to be such a man.

Gevri struggled to keep his voice low and controlled. He stood and picked up Amma's book. "Father, there is no honor in what you're planning to do in the morning. Deep down, you must know that."

"What do you know of honor, boy?" the general whispered.

"An honorable path has been opened to you, Father. We're all counting on you to take it." He turned to leave the tent.

"Dismissed!" the general called after him.

Gevri couldn't sleep that night; he doubted anyone could, not even Jix. When the soft light of the morning and birdsong finally came, a solemn dread came along with it.

True to his word, the general strode out to the ridge at first light. Behind the wagons and carts that served as a flimsy barricade, some of the people stood bravely at the front of the crowd, hands clasped and heads held high. Taemon and Amma were among them.

The general did not ask Gevri to amplify his voice this time, but there was no need. Everyone quieted to hear the general. "Taemon Houser! People of Deliverance!" His voice boomed across the dewy grass that separated the two groups. "What is your decision? Will you join us against the Nau, or will you be destroyed this day?"

All eyes and ears were on Taemon. Gevri barely noticed Jix nuzzling his hand or Berliott tugging at his sleeve.

"Sir," Berliott whispered, "something's coming."

Gevri grunted softly, patting Jix absently.

"It's coming in fast, sir," she said.

"What is?"

Berliott started to answer, but Taemon's reply cut her off.

"Our choice is this," Taemon said. He wasn't amplifying his voice either, which made Gevri think the psi blocker was still working. "We choose to honor Nathan's agreement with the Heart of the Earth, that psi will not be used to destroy humankind. We call upon you to honor that choice."

"Be it so," said the general. He raised one arm. "Take aim!"

A cacophony of sounds erupted. From the Republikites, the metallic sounds of guns readying to fire; the treads of the tanks grinding, moving into position, their turrets rotating as they took aim at the enemy. From the Nathanites, crying, shouting, screaming. But there was something else, a sound that sent fear racing through Gevri's veins.

He turned to Berliott. "Copters?"

She nodded. "The Nau are coming."

Gevri stood up and shouted this time: "Copters!"

The heads of all the soldiers snapped upward, searching the sky.

A moment later, they appeared: Nau copters swooping overhead. They strafed the soldiers at the front of the lines, the bullets driving the soldiers back.

"Retreat!" called the general into the radio. "Into the trees for cover!"

Jix ran ahead. Gevri called his archons into a tight formation, then exercised dominion to create a shield that covered them, just as he had done when they escaped from the prison. "Stay close," he told them, "and follow Jix."

Gevri saw a tank explode. The copters weren't just spitting bullets; they were firing missiles, too! The turrets on the tanks and war machines couldn't rotate quickly enough to sight the planes, and one by one, they were destroyed by the Nau.

"How did they know about Deliverance?" Saunch said. "How did they know we'd be here?"

Gevri had no answers. But he knew one thing: "This changes everything."

NAU MILITARY INTEL ADMIN LOGBOOK

> Enemy Engagement Report from Spec Ops Command Unit
#278: Confirmed targets destroyed: 18 Republik war
machines, 34 Republik tanks, unknown number of enemy
personnel. Engagement is ongoing. Updates to follow. <

24 TAEMON

Taemon watched, awestruck, as the Nau flying machines worked their destruction on the army of the Republik. In a matter of minutes, the tanks and war machines were torn to shreds, and the soldiers had hightailed it into the woods. Maybe this is what the Heart of the Earth had in mind the entire time: the Nau would destroy the Republikite army and all the archons, thereby wiping all psionic power from the face of the earth.

The noise died down eventually, and Taemon wasn't sure what came next. Was the battle over? Or, as General

Sarin had warned, were the Nau here to take over Deliverance?

Amma turned to Taemon. "What's happening?" she asked.

"I'm not sure," Taemon said. "I'd feel a lot better about this if I could get rid of the psi blocker."

The whining roar of the flying machines returned as they circled gracefully toward the earth. Taemon had never seen such machines before. Huge propeller blades whirred on their tops, allowing them to fly and even to hover. Enormous guns stuck out in every direction, operated by soldiers hidden inside.

The machines hovered over the beach grass before slowly lowering to the ground—first one, then three more, then five more, until nine of these huge flying machines had landed in the grass between the beach and the trees. The second they touched the ground, the bellies of the machines opened and a ramp slid out of each of them. Soldiers poured out. Taemon couldn't help but admire the way they efficiently positioned themselves around the cluster of machines. When the formation was complete, a tall man stepped out of the ramp of one of the planes. His uniform was the same drab gray as the soldiers' uniforms, but he had burgundy trim on his sleeves. Clearly this man was important.

Another soldier handed the officer a short stick of some kind. The man raised it to his mouth and spoke into it. As he did so, his voice became amplified.

"The people of Deliverance and the army of the Republik will each send one spokesman to discuss the terms of their surrender."

Taemon and Amma exchanged a look. "Surrender as in no more fighting? Or surrender as in . . . something else?" Taemon asked.

"I don't know."

Taemon turned to Hannova, wondering if she would prefer to be their spokesperson. But she shook her head, her expression serious. It needed to be him. He knew it — even if he wished otherwise.

Amma gave him a steady look. He wanted her to come with him, wanted her to tell him everything would be fine. But she couldn't promise that any more than he could.

She took his hand, leaned forward, and kissed his cheek. "Do what you have to," she whispered.

Taemon nodded. He turned and walked toward the Nau leader. It was a long walk.

General Sarin walked from the other direction. Taemon reached the Nau leader first, but the man in the gray coat said nothing until General Sarin arrived.

"My name is Commander U. Felmark Puster. I represent the Nau nations and have been given final authority to deal with this situation. Our mission is to address the psychic aberration known as psi, or dominion. The Nau have determined that this aberration causes chaos and interferes with the natural order of human civilization. It is not predictable enough or scientific enough to be used in any productive way. Therefore, I have been given the charge to eradicate it."

"That is not within your power," General Sarin said.

Commander Puster's expression was stony. "I assure you, it most certainly is."

"If I may speak, sir," said Taemon. "I have already dealt with this matter in our society. Psi no longer exists among our people. It has been, as you say, eradicated."

"You still have it," the general said.

"Is this true?" Commander Puster asked.

"Yes," Taemon said. "But I am the only one. No one else in Deliverance has any psionic powers."

The commander checked a dial strapped to his wrist. "It seems you are telling the truth," he said.

Taemon wondered what kind of dial could tell him that, but it wasn't a question he dared to ask.

"And you, General Sarin, how many of your soldiers have the aberration you call dominion?"

The general stiffened his back. "I refuse to answer that question."

"Let me explain to you how this is going to work," said Commander Puster. "We intend to kill every person who has psi or dominion. If you cooperate, we will spare those who do not. If you fight us, we will simply kill all of you. Now, my information is that only a small part of your army has these so-called powers. If you turn them over to me, I am authorized to allow the rest of your soldiers to leave peacefully."

General Sarin opened his mouth to reply, but Commander Puster cut him off. "Do not try to deceive us, General. We will check each one of your soldiers to assure no one with these powers is spared."

Taemon felt sick to his stomach. If they planned to kill everyone who had psi, that meant hundreds of young archons would die, and one Nathanite—himself. But it also meant that everyone else in Deliverance would be free, and they would be free from the threat of an archon army.

Is this what you had in mind? Taemon asked the Heart of the Earth. *This is your solution?*

"We will surrender," General Sarin said, surprising Taemon. "We will turn over all our weapons, if, in return, you allow all our people to live. Archons included."

"There will be no negotiation, General. As we speak, our sensors indicate that your archons are trying to attack our copters, to tear them apart. But they cannot do it. These copters are equipped with cloaking devices that render destruction by telekinesis impossible. However, we cannot refit our entire military to account for this contingency. It is much more cost efficient to simply eradicate this ability. It's unfortunate that you did not eliminate this evil from your society as the people of Nathan have."

Things were starting to connect in Taemon's mind. "Commander Puster, sir, are you aware that there are several other forms of dominion in addition to telekinesis?"

The commander frowned. "Certainly. Our study of Lieutenant Sarin and his unit has yielded much data."

"So you have ways to counteract those powers?" Taemon asked.

The commander narrowed his eyes. "What are you implying?"

"Nothing, sir," Taemon said. "I am just impressed by your people's ingenuity. I thought the Republikite army were the only ones who had managed to block psionic abilities."

The commander held his gaze for a moment longer, and Taemon wondered if he'd tipped his hand. But soon Commander Puster turned back to General Sarin to reiterate the details of his plan.

Taemon felt confident that whatever cloaking device was protecting these flying machines—these copters—it was protecting them only from telekinesis. If he could get General Sarin to unblock his psi, he could use clairvoyance to get past the cloaking devices and destroy the machines. He was sure of it.

NAU MILITARY INTEL ADMIN LOGBOOK

> Enemy Engagement Report from Technical Support
attached to Spec Ops Command Unit #278: Cloaking devices
performed as expected to prevent psychic aggression and/
or destruction of property. The size of the device does
not seem to be an issue. Large and small devices are
equally effective. <

25 GEVRI

One of the archons had gotten ahold of a pair of binoculars, and Gevri used them to watch his father. He nearly threw up when he saw U. Felmark Puster step out of the helicopter. The monster. What were they talking about? What in the world was going on?

Jix paced in a tight circle again.

Gevri was beside himself. He wished he knew some way to use dominion to eavesdrop, but telepathy didn't work that way. *What are you saying?*

"There's something really strange about those copters," Wendomer said.

Gevri turned the binoculars to the helicopters but didn't see anything amiss. "What do you mean?"

"My eyes tell me what they look like, but when I use clairvoyance, I see something different."

"Something's off for me, too," said Berliott. "I think that's why I didn't notice them until they were so close."

"That, and we weren't really searching the skies," Pik said.

"Something's weird, all right," Gevri said. "If I try to use dominion to pull a piece off a copter, it doesn't work. I can't disassemble their guns, either. Must be some kind of blocking device."

Saunch shook his head. "It doesn't feel like a blocking device."

"What else could it be?" Gevri asked, still peering at the copter through the binoculars.

"Somehow they're making the copters look different from what they are," Wendomer said.

"Gods," Gevri whispered. "It's not a blocking device—it's a cloaking device." He lowered the binoculars and scrambled for a scrap of paper and pencil in his equipment bag. When he found them, he gave them to Wendomer. "You have clairvoyance, and I have telekinesis. I need you to draw what you see. If I can visualize it well enough, I can use telekinesis to disable the helicopters."

Wendomer looked confused. "You want me to draw?"

"Yes, and hurry!"

The young archon snapped into action and started to sketch. Gevri watched over her shoulder. The drawing was much too vague. "No, no! It has to be precise."

"I'm not much good at drawing, sir," Wendomer said. She tried to erase something, but the smudge made it worse.

"Okay," Gevri said. "Just do your best."

Wendomer nodded and turned back to her drawing, scowling with concentration.

Gevri jiggled his knee impatiently. Wendomer's drawing wasn't going to help. Gevri would never be able to picture the machine clearly enough to use dominion. His ability was strong enough, but that visual connection was absolutely vital. A smudgy sketch just wasn't going to cut it.

Gevri grabbed the binoculars and peered at Taemon, the general, and Puster. They were still talking. For the thousandth time, Gevri wished he had clairvoyance along with his telekinesis, as Taemon did. There would be almost nothing he couldn't do. He could take those helicopters apart in a heartbeat.

An idea hit him like a brick in the head. "Saunch, who has the remote for the psi blocking device?"

Saunch shrugged. "I saw the general slip it into his pocket this morning, sir."

"All right, if we can't get to the remote, we'll go after the device itself."

Jix finally stopped pacing and sat down facing the Nathanites.

Gevri turned the binoculars toward the Nathanites. Everyone in the crowd looked confused, all eyes on Taemon as he spoke to the Nau commander. Gevri continued to scan the crowd. *Now, where is that scarlet silk tunic? Yes. Right there.*

He could do this next part himself, but Jix would do it so much better. He leaned down until his chin nearly rested on top of the jaguar's head. "See that boy over there, Jix?" Gevri whispered. "The one in red?"

Jix made her soft chuffing noise.

"I want you to send him a telepathic message. Put the

fear of the gods in him. Make him turn and run toward the ocean. Not *into* the ocean, mind you, but make him run as far from Taemon as he can get. We need to get the blocking device out of range."

Gevri stood up again and trained his binoculars on Yens. The shocked look on Yens's face was the funniest thing he'd seen in months. Yens looked around, then ran wildly toward the shore, scarlet silk flapping.

"What did you do?" Saunch asked.

"We just gave Taemon his psi back," Gevri said. "Now let's see what he does with it."

Jix made a sound that Gevri could have sworn sounded like a chuckle.

NAU MILITARY INTEL ADMIN LOGBOOK

> Enemy Engagement Update from Spec Ops Command
Unit #278: Enemy personnel subdued. Commander Puster
currently engaging enemy authorities in verbal
negotiations. Situation under control. Updates to follow. <

26 TAEMON

Taemon had decided that Commander Puster liked hearing himself talk. He was yammering about analysis and data and research when it was clear that he had made up his mind. He was going to kill everyone with any kind of psychic power. Taemon suspected the general knew it, too. This would not end well.

As Taemon was coming to that conclusion, the pain in his head began to let up. In a few more seconds, it was gone completely. The psi blocker was gone! He looked to the general, wondering how he'd known that this was what was needed. But if the general had just acted to save Taemon and his people, his face gave nothing away.

No matter. The time for jolly-jawing was over.

With clairvoyance, Taemon could see what the commander's flying machine really looked like, not just the image that the cloaking device somehow projected. Without moving a muscle, Taemon began ripping the Nau machine apart, starting with the guns.

At the first sound of wrenching metal, the commander turned. "No!"

The soldier who stood guard near the commander swung his gun this way and that. "Who do I shoot?"

"Shoot them all!" yelled the commander, but the general was too quick. Already he had wrestled the gun away from the soldier and began shooting Nau soldiers, starting with Commander Puster, who fell to the ground.

Taemon used psi to deflect the bullets headed his way and disassemble all the guns, then turned his attention back to the flying machines. As fast as he was working to pull things apart with telekinesis, it wasn't fast enough. The machines that were still intact were lifting off one by one, swinging into position to kill the crowds in the most efficient way.

"Take cover!" Taemon yelled at the thousands of terrified faces. "Everyone get down!" Almost in unison they crouched down and covered their heads.

General Sarin grabbed Taemon's arm. "Do something!" he commanded. "You're the only one who can save us!"

Taemon locked the general in his gaze. This was the man who had led the army that had been poised to eliminate the people of Deliverance just minutes ago. Why should Taemon help this Republikite?

Because this is how the True Son unites a nation. The voice of the Heart of the Earth echoed in his mind.

Taemon clasped the general's shoulder. The two stood eye to eye. "After today," Taemon said, "our people will be united again. We will either live together or we will die together."

"Yes," the general said.

"There is a price that must be paid," Taemon said. "You must relinquish all claims to dominion. Our two nations cannot be one with the imbalance caused by dominion."

The general nodded. "Be it so."

Bowing his head, Taemon reached out to the Heart of the Earth.

I'm ready to do what needs to be done. If I have to give my life, I will do it. Please, help me to protect these people. Don't abandon us now.

The solution came to him in a clear image. He knew exactly what to do and how to do it. He swept away his fear and got to work.

He gathered a tremendous amount of psi, more than he had ever used before. It flowed through him like a flood rushing through a canyon. It grew and grew until he felt he was floating outside his body. His knees buckled and his body swayed, but he felt the general bracing him up.

First he used the psi he had gathered to fling each one of the flying machines far into the ocean. He knew without having to use clairvoyance that they were equipped with life rafts. The soldiers would be unharmed.

But that was only the beginning. What he planned to do next would require every psionic ability he had.

"Tell your soldiers to gather at the beach," Taemon said to the general. "I need them out of the woods. And no guns. Have them leave their guns behind."

"Why?" General Sarin asked. "You've gotten rid of the Nau."

"There is a price that must be paid. Just tell everyone to

gather at the beach." Taemon looked him in the eye, and the general dared not argue. He let go of Taemon's arm and made the call on his radio.

When the people of Deliverance saw the soldiers running toward them, they started to panic. Taemon amplified his voice and spoke to them.

"Do not be afraid," he said. "Today is the day that the people of Nathan return to their lands in peace."

That seemed to calm things down. Taemon knelt and closed his fists around the dirt and pebbles at his feet.

Once again, he summoned forth all the psi he could and drew it into himself. It swelled and swirled inside him, waiting for his direction. Still he gathered more power, and more, until he was no longer himself. He was the soil and the grass, the trees and the mountains themselves. He called on psychometry, connecting with the rocks he held in his hands. He saw the history of this land, what it had looked like before Nathan had summoned rock and earth from far below the surface and called it forth to create the mountains. With clairvoyance, he surveyed the land in all its detail. He perceived every sand dune, every cliff, every meadow, every river and boulder and tree. He held it all in one grand vision. He used remote viewing to stretch this awareness all the way from the beach where he stood to the peak of Mount Deliverance and all its sister mountains. All the way from the sea on the north to the sea on the south. The entire peninsula that was the land of Deliverance. All of this he held in his mind.

You will reshape yourself, he told the land, *as I direct you.*

A crack formed at the base of Mount Deliverance. It lengthened and widened, the earth rumbling beneath it. As the chasm grew wider, the mountain began to crumble. Rocks and boulders fell and filled it. Taemon used all the energy in the cyclone of psi that raged inside him and directed it into the earth. *Open, open. Wider, wider.*

The great chasm lengthened along the mountain range. Taemon made sure to direct it away from where the people had gathered on the beach.

Open, open, Taemon urged. *Wider, wider.*

The earth groaned and rumbled. The noise was incredible as the gap in the earth's surface grew wider still.

Now Taemon directed his psi toward the great mountains. *Lower. Sink into the earth from which you once sprang. Lower, lower.* Taemon showed the land what he needed it to do. *Lower. Smoother. Flatter.*

The psi poured in him and from him and never seemed

to deplete itself. Taemon had to use every bit of strength to harness it. He had to direct it, show it what to do, and keep a clear vision in his head. It obeyed without fail.

When the vision in his eyes matched the vision in his head, Taemon knew his work was finished. The price that had to be paid was the mountains. The Heart of the Earth had given the mountains to Nathan's people long ago, as protection against their enemies. In return, Nathan's people had agreed to use psi for good. When Nathan's people became greedy and started finding ways to get around the boundaries and rules of psi, their agreement with the Heart of the Earth was broken. And since that promise was broken, the earth had taken the mountains unto herself once again. The mountains of Deliverance were gone. In their place was smooth, fertile land. It was up to both peoples to unite themselves and live in peace once again.

Taemon would miss the mountains and the woods and the rivers of Deliverance, but it was a fair price for the lives of thousands of people, and he had paid it.

NAU MILITARY INTEL ADMIN LOGBOOK

> Enemy Engagement Report: Heavy losses in Foreign
Sector #083 [aka The Republik]. Data remain
unconfirmed. <

> Military Personnel Status Update: Commander U. Felmark
Puster [ID# 229-8831-305] unaccounted for following enemy
engagement in Foreign Sector #083. <

> Bureau of Geographic Surveys Report: Highly unusual
geographic shifts confirmed in Foreign Sector #083
[aka The Republik]. Entire region may be unsafe.
Recommendation: Cease all military activity in Foreign
Sector #083. <

> Recommendation approved. <

> Enemy Engagement Report: Strong aberrant psychic
aggression confirmed in Foreign Sector #083. All other
data unconfirmed. Activity in this region is deemed
highly dangerous to all personnel. Recommendations:
(1 of 2) Cease all military activity in Foreign Sector
#083. (2 of 2) Reclassify Foreign Sector #083 to Area of
No Interest. <

> Recommendations (1 of 2) and (2 of 2) approved. <

27 AMMA

It was four o'clock in the afternoon, and Amma walked briskly to Drigg's workshop. When she opened the door, Drigg looked up from the saw he was sharpening. He started to say something, but Amma put her finger to her mouth.

Drigg gave her a wry smile, pointed to the opposite end of the workshop, then turned back to his saw.

Amma tiptoed around large gears and half-assembled engines, a stack of tires and a byrider helmet.

There he was, lying on the floor next to an old byrider. She watched him for a moment, his face tensed with deep concentration, the tip of his tongue pressed against his upper lip. He looked thoroughly happy, he and his new byrider. New *old* byrider.

"What is it with you and engines?" Amma said.

He dropped his wrench, which made her laugh.

She brushed some grit from the cement floor and sat down next to him. "First you take them apart, then you put them together, then you take them apart again."

Taemon shrugged. "I guess I just like to see how things fit together. I like to see if I can make them work better."

His words struck her as profound. That was exactly what he'd done to Deliverance—he'd taken it apart and put it back together.

Taemon picked up his wrench again, and Amma watched him work for a few minutes. He certainly had seen how all the parts of Deliverance had fit together. He'd known there was something wrong before anyone else did. And he fixed it. Things were finally getting better in Deliverance. Better than Amma could ever have imagined. People were learning new trades and building new houses. Commerce had begun, with goods being traded back and forth between Deliverance and the Republik.

And Taemon had changed Kanjai, too. It was no longer a military outpost, but a community dedicated to industry.

She watched him fiddle with some little whatzie-thingy on the byrider. He struggled with it for a minute, but he never used psi. He still had it, but she hadn't seen him use it since the day he'd pulled the mountains down.

"Do you ever think about using psi?" Amma asked. "Does it bother you that you still have it?"

Taemon paused for a moment. He had a charming little smudge of grease just next to his nose. "No, it doesn't bother me."

"Do you think you'll ever use it again?"

He shrugged. "Not unless there's a really good reason to."

"But it doesn't bother you like it used to."

Taemon gave the wrench a couple of firm twists. "I guess I'm not afraid anymore. For a long time, I was terrified I'd do something awful with psi. But now I feel like I've finally proved to the Heart of the Earth I won't do anything terrible with psi."

"And proved it to yourself," Amma said.

"That, too." Taemon reached over and grabbed a rag to wipe the grease off his wrench. "I'm just about done here. Then I'll get cleaned up."

"Perfect," Amma said. "I want to show you something."

A few minutes later, Amma led Taemon to a vacant lot near the edge of the colony. She spread her arms in a grand gesture. "Look! Isn't it beautiful?"

Taemon rubbed his chin. "Cha, sure. Um, what is it?"

"It's a library!" Amma couldn't stop herself from spinning in a little circle. She'd dreamed about this for so long.

"Really?" Taemon said.

"Yes." She took his hand and led him forward a few more steps. "Da and Abson and Rhody are going to pour the foundation next week. See those stakes? That's one corner of the building." She pulled him in the opposite direction. He ran to keep up with her.

"And here's the other corner. And this . . ." Amma changed directions again. "This is where the front door will be."

Taemon pantomimed opening the front door. He held it open, bowed deeply, and held out his arm. "After you, Miss Parvel."

Amma laughed and pretended to step inside the invisible library. He followed her, making a point to shut the door. Taking him by the shoulders, she positioned him just so. "We're in the foyer now. And right there, hung on the wall in a prominent place, can you see it?"

"Um. Almost. It's . . . uh . . . it's a picture?" Taemon guessed.

Amma smiled. "Wrong. It's in a frame, but it's not a picture. It's your treaty, silly."

Taemon sighed, his shoulder sagging. "Oh, no. Don't call it that. It's not my treaty."

"Of course it is," Amma said. "They named it after you."

"I wish they hadn't." Taemon frowned and looked at his shoes. "A lot of people worked on that, not just me."

"Hoy, Taemon. Give yourself a little credit. You did some pretty amazing things."

"Plenty of people are doing amazing things. Da is leading the church now. You're building a library. Yens is putting together a new sports league. Even Gevri is contributing. He was here just last week working with Solovar and Hannova on the trade agreements."

"But we wouldn't be doing these things if it hadn't been for you," Amma said. "Now, Mr. Houser, shall we continue our official tour of the library?" She hooked her arm in his elbow and walked him through the grass. "On your left, you will see the historical collection of books once assembled by the prophet Nathan himself. These books were cared for meticulously by the Parvels, a prestigious family in the colony. Legend has it that they were stolen by none other than Yens Houser, taken to the fabled Temple of Deliverance, then stolen a second time and taken to Kanjai. Now they have been returned and assembled once again in the special collection you see before you."

"Wow," Taemon whispered. "Won't that be something? I can't wait to see it."

She took hold of his arms and turned him around. "And on this side is a large room where classes are taught by Amma Parvel, the famous educator known for her intellect and wisdom."

Taemon grinned. "And humility."

"And humility," she repeated.

"And beauty."

"And . . ." Amma couldn't quite bring herself to repeat that. After all this time, after everything they'd been through, there had always been an understanding between them. They never talked about it, but Amma had always felt that their friendship would become something more. In the three years they had known each other, there had always been some crisis, some huge problem that had to be solved. Amma had always hoped that maybe, when things calmed down, or when they were older, she and Taemon would be more than friends.

Maybe that time was now.

She looked away from Taemon and turned her gaze toward the vast plains, now covered with new grass. She tried to pick the spot where the peak of Mount Deliverance used to be. Maybe just . . . there.

She felt Taemon's arm around her shoulders. "I hope you're going to put windows on this side of the library."

"That's a good idea," she said. "People can come here and look out over the Plains of Deliverance." She sighed contentedly. "So, Mr. Knife, any regrets?" she asked.

Taemon was quiet for a moment. "I'll always miss the mountain," he said. "But I think we've gained much more than we lost." His eyes held hers. "I know *I* have."

She smiled and slipped her arm around his waist. "Me, too," she said. "Me, too."

ACKNOWLEDGMENTS

So many wonderful people have helped me tell Taemon's story: My fabulous agent, Molly Jaffa, connected with Taemon right away and never doubted; the marvelous Kaylan Adair not only knew how to get the manuscript in shape, but also knew how to nurture me as a writer. Thank you to all the young readers who told me how much they loved *Freakling* and *Archon* and urged me to write another book as quickly as I could. I will always treasure the authorial kinship of the people from Richmond Children's Writers: Hazel Buys, Deb Dudley, Dan Elasky, Troy Howell, Marianne McKee, Stephanie McPherson, Brian Rock, and Chris Sorensen. Thanks to everyone at James River Writers: Bill and Sheri Blume, Katharine Herndon, Kristi Tuck-Austin, Leila Gaskin, David Kazzie, Erica Orloff, Gigi Amateau, Meg Medina, Anne Westrick, Julie Geen, Mike and Shawna Christos, Kris Spisak, Jon Sealy, Josh Cane, Vernon Wildy, Joanna Lee, Robin Farmer, Charles Genera, and so many others who make it possible for writers to learn from writers. I am grateful to the wonderful staff at bbgb bookstore, who work to get great books in the hands of kids, and to the many amazing librarians who use their passion for books to nurture a new generation of readers. Most of all, thanks to my family: Kip, Callie, Ben, Julie, Tim, Savanna, and Magnus — because everything is better with them in my life.